So

"I don't mind telling you I'm a little shook up.

"Yesterday morning, my life was on a nice, even, predictable course. Now I don't know where I'm going."

"I can tell you where you're going," Dak replied. "You don't think you can walk away from that kiss last night, do you?"

"No," Kathy admitted shakily.

"Then, where you're going is right back into my arms to take up where we left off. Why did you run away like that?"

"You know good and well why," she said huskily. "A few more minutes and we would have passed the point of no return."

Dak chuckled. "That would have been so bad?"

"No," she murmured. "It wouldn't have been so bad at all. But I'm not going to run back into your arms, Dak. Not after what happened between us in the past."

Dear Reader:

The spirit of the Silhouette Romance Homecoming Celebration lives on as each month we bring you six books by continuing stars!

And we have a galaxy of stars planned for 1988. In the coming months, we're publishing romances by many of your favorite authors such as Annette Broadrick, Sondra Stanford and Brittany Young. Beginning in January, Debbie Macomber has written a trilogy designed to cure any midwinter blues. And that's not all—during the summer, Diana Palmer presents her most engaging heroes and heroines in a trilogy that will be sure to capture your heart.

Your response to these authors and other authors of Silhouette Romances has served as a touchstone for us, and we're pleased to bring you more books with Silhouette's distinctive medley of charm, wit and—above all—romance.

I hope you enjoy this book and the many stories to come. Come home to romance—for always!

Sincerely,

Tara Hughes
Senior Editor
Silhouette Books

PATTI BECKMAN

Someday
My Love

Silhouette *Romance*

Published by Silhouette Books New York

America's Publisher of Contemporary Romance

SILHOUETTE BOOKS
300 E. 42nd St., New York, N.Y. 10017

Copyright © 1988 by Charles and Patti Boeckman, Inc.

ISBN: 0-373-08571-0

First Silhouette Books printing April 1988

America's Publisher of Contemporary Romance

Printed in the U.S.A.

Books by Patti Beckman

Silhouette Romance

Captive Heart #8
The Beachcomber #37
Louisiana Lady #54
Angry Lover #72
Love's Treacherous Journey #96
Spotlight to Fame #124
Daring Encounter #154
Mermaid's Touch #179
Forbidden Affair #227
Time for Us #273
On Stage #348
Someday My Love #571

Silhouette Special Edition

Bitter Victory #13
Tender Deception #61
Enchanted Surrender #85
Thunder at Dawn #109
Storm Over the Everglades #169
Nashville Blues #212
The Movie #226
Odds Against Tomorrow #270
Dateline: Washington #278
Summer's Storm #321
Danger in His Arms #370

PATTI BECKMAN

has lived the exciting lives of many of her heroines. She has been an actress, airline pilot, author and bass player in her husband's jazz band. Her interesting locales and spirited characters will delight her reading audience. She lives with her husband, Charles, and daughter along the coast of Texas.

Chapter One

In that split second between life and death, Kathy Ayers reacted instinctively. Her reflexes trained and sure, she jammed her right foot down on the brake pedal with all her might.

Her small car skidded to a stop in a cloud of dust. For an awful moment she sat frozen, her white-knuckled fingers gripping the steering wheel. There was an empty pit where her stomach should have been.

Barely a dozen feet from her front bumper stood the boy, freckles like sprinkled cinnamon across his white face, his body rigid with startled fright, his blue eyes wide and staring.

Suddenly angry, she grabbed the door handle with trembling fingers, threw it open and jumped out. "You crazy kid!" she exploded. "You ran right in front of my car! I nearly killed you."

The fright in the boy's blue eyes changed to defiance. He squared his shoulders and raised his chin, challenging her with his gaze. "Couldn't help it. They were after me."

"Who was after you?"

Now that she had a better look at him, Kathy saw the youngster couldn't have been more than seven or eight. His blue jeans and Western boots looked dusty but new. In this southern Texas town of Endless, population six thousand, Kathy knew most of the kids in town. She didn't know this one whose fair skin had not been exposed to the hot Texas sun long enough yet to tan, and, whose jeans and boots had not been broken in.

"Stranger in these parts, aren't you?"

The boy shrugged.

She continued to study him. Something about him bothered her, tugged at some distant, half-forgotten memory. She was sure she'd never seen him around town before, and yet something about his curly blond hair, the lines of his jaw and lips evoked a vague, disturbing emotion.

Kathy repeated her first question. "Who was after you?"

His blue eyes looked at her, then turned away. "Aliens."

"Oh." She nibbled thoughtfully at her bottom lip. "Spaceship?"

He nodded.

She struggled to maintain a serious expression. Her fright and anger were giving way to amusement. "What's your name?"

"Joedy."

"That's a nice name."

"It's all right, I guess."

She glanced around them. They were on the outskirts of town. There was a scattering of buildings typical of a South Texas ranching community—a feed store, garage, welding shop and a Dairy Queen. The streets were quiet, and no one was on the sidewalks. This time of the morning the Dairy Queen had just opened but wasn't doing any business yet.

Her gaze swung back to the boy. "Where are your parents, Joedy?"

He shrugged one shoulder. "Guess the aliens took 'em." Defiance and rebellion radiated out from the rigid stiffness in his slender body.

Kathy looked at him thoughtfully, trying not to grin. Her experience as a courtroom lawyer had trained her to deal with hostile witnesses. A disarming smile spread over her face. She glanced at the Dairy Queen and then back to him. "Hey, how would you like some ice cream, Joedy?"

His eyes wavered.

"They've got a terrific way of dipping a cone in chocolate. Bet you'd like one of those."

"Well...."

Kathy parked her car at the side of the street, then walked to the Dairy Queen with the boy. Standing outside the drive-in window, they ordered two ice-cream cones dipped in chocolate, then sat down at one of the nearby picnic tables.

"Did the aliens take your parents into the space-ship, Joedy?"

"Uh-huh."

She looked at him gravely. "Guess we ought to report this to the space agency—they like to know about things like this. They'll want a description. What did your parents look like?"

"Just my dad," Joedy said between bites. "My mom's in heaven." He stopped eating for a moment, his eyes clouding. Then he went back to devouring the ice cream in silence.

Kathy looked at him thoughtfully. "Well, tell me about your dad, Joedy. What's his name?"

The question was never answered; a pickup truck had turned a corner and driven toward them. It came to a stop at the curb across the street and the tall, broad-shouldered driver stepped from the cab and crossed toward them in a few long-legged strides.

At first all Kathy noticed was that he was typically dressed in blue jeans and boots. A large man, he had the trim, muscular lines of an athlete and curly blond hair like the boy.

Then he drew closer and her heart lurched. She sat very still, her thought processes suddenly stilled. A feeling of unreality gripped her.

Dimly she was aware of the boy getting up from the table and starting to move away, stopping when the man put a broad hand on his shoulder.

To Kathy, the man said, "Sorry, Ma'am." The man apologized to Kathy. "I hope the boy hasn't been a bother to you..."

His voice faded.

They stood there looking at each other, the years drifting away like wisps of fog. Kathy saw in his surprised eyes the emotions that she knew must be reflected in hers—the old tenderness, old heartbreak...the old hurt and anger. They were feelings that had been locked away along with yellowed newspaper clippings, a battered high school yearbook, a dusty corsage....

"Kathy," he said slowly, as if trying to convince himself it was really she. "Kathy Ayers!"

Then the memory of his betrayal so many years before flared like burning coals long buried under cold ashes. "Hello, Dak," she said coldly.

Why should she be so dazed, so surprised? She had heard several weeks ago that he was back, that he had, in fact, bought the old Burkshire place adjacent to her land. It was inevitable that she would run into him sooner or later, an event that she'd anticipated with a great deal of uneasiness. Painful emotion she had expected, but she had not been prepared for their overwhelming intensity after such a long time.

"I—I heard you had moved back," she said stiffly.

He nodded. "Yeah." He smiled wryly. "Guess I got homesick for the warmth of small-town friendliness. And I thought a change would be good for Joedy." He tousled the boy's hair affectionately but kept a grip on his son's arm.

There was a moment of awkward silence as the air crackled with churning emotions.

Dak looked down at the boy. "I don't know what I'm going to do with you, Joedy. You run away like that again, I'm going to have to give you a paddling." He glanced at Kathy with an expression of frustration and embarrassment. "Sorry about

Joedy," he apologized. "We drove in early this morning. I was doing some grocery shopping.... Turned my back and Joedy had vanished."

Now she understood why the boy had looked so familiar. He was obviously Dak's son; the resemblance was unmistakable. Joedy had the same unruly blond hair, same deep blue eyes, same strong, determined chin.

She drew a deep breath, making an effort to keep her emotions from getting the best of her voice. "We were getting along fine." She smiled faintly at Joedy. "He was trying to get away from the aliens."

Dak sighed. "Joedy, where do you get those wild ideas?"

The boy was looking defiant again. "There *were* aliens. They came in a spaceship."

Dak looked apologetically at Kathy. "He's been having a rough time of it since his mother died last year."

Kathy remembered the look on Joedy's face when he had said his mother was in heaven. She'd heard that Dak had married a movie starlet after he moved to California and that she'd been killed in an accident on a set last year. Gossip like that inevitably drifted back to this community where Dak had once been the town hero. A town like Endless didn't spawn many celebrities and Dak had once put the place on the map. People here hadn't forgotten the time the big-city reporters and the national network TV news teams had come to Endless when Dak Roberts won the Olympic medal. Since then, his fame had been kept alive with TV commercials and a syndicated half-hour physical fitness program. Dak was the local boy who had made good, who had become a national celebrity.

She had tried not to pay attention to the gossip that filtered back after Dak went to California, but how could she avoid wondering what became of the man who had been her first love, and then had betrayed her so cruelly? Dak Roberts had been a chapter of her life that she had not easily forgotten.

"I...guess we're kind of neighbors," Dak said. "I bought the old Burkshire place. I understand my northeast pasture abuts your ranch."

"So I've heard," she replied coldly. It would have been civil of her to murmur some kind of polite welcome, but she couldn't bring herself to be that hypocritical. "I have to get to work."

She turned to leave, but Dak's son took a quick step toward her. He was clutching his half-eaten ice-cream cone, looking at her in a strangely intense way. "Thanks for the ice cream," he mumbled.

She smiled at him. "You're very welcome, Joedy." Without thinking, she reached out and wiped a smear of chocolate from the corner of his lip. "You be a good boy, now."

His blue eyes looked directly at her. He didn't look like an angry, rebellious boy now. What she saw in those blue eyes was loneliness and sadness. She felt a sudden urge to take him in her arms and mother him. No matter how she felt about Dak, she had formed an instant attachment to the boy.

Apparently the feeling was mutual. "Maybe you could come see me sometime?" Joedy asked wistfully.

She smiled fondly. "I—I don't know...."

"Dad bought me a horse. I'll let you ride her."

His blue eyes were pleading, almost desperate.

"Well...we'll see, Joedy."

She glanced up at Dak. The warm, soft feelings that Joedy had evoked became chilled. Her gaze turned cold and bitter. She turned and walked quickly to her car.

Kathy drove to the center of town where a new professional office building, the Kline Building, had been constructed last year. She took the self-service elevator to the third floor, and walked down the hall to the suite of offices with Katherine Ayers, Attorney at Law stenciled on the door.

Her secretary, Millie Thompson, had arrived only a few minutes before. She was a pleasant, middle-aged woman with a bright personality. After she had raised her children, Millie had refreshed her secretarial skills and had gone looking for a job. Kathy had hired her a year ago and had been glad ever since that she did.

When Kathy walked in, the first thing she saw were election campaign posters and bumper stickers piled on chairs and stacked around the wall. Elect Kathy Ayers Mayor, proclaimed large red and blue posters. Kathy's The One For Us! exclaimed equally colorful bumper stickers.

"Good morning, Millie," Kathy greeted.

"Morning, Kathy."

"When did those arrive?" Kathy asked, nodding at the campaign material.

"Late yesterday, after you left. I didn't know what to do with them, so I piled them around here. Arthur Peters is coming by sometime this morning to take them over to the campaign headquarters."

"Well, the colors are loud enough," Kathy muttered, embarrassed at the blatant display. "But I guess that's what it takes to get elected."

She strode into her spacious office. One wall was lined with mahogany bookshelves filled with her extensive law library. Against another wall was an antique rolltop desk that had once been in her grandfather's law office. Above it hung a large portrait of her father, Burke Ayers, characteristically attired in his ranching clothes. It was a no-nonsense, forthright portrait of a strong man with piercing black eyes and steel gray hair, his features lined and leathery from the ruthless sun and scorching winds of a Texas ranch.

Behind Kathy's expansive desk was a picture window overlooking the roofs of the town and the chaparral-dotted ranchland beyond that dissolved in a blue haze on the horizon.

The only sound in the deserted offices was the soft murmur from the air-conditioning ducts, already turned on to battle the midsummer heat.

Kathy dropped her briefcase on her desk. It was quiet now, but soon the phone would start ringing and there would be a steady stream of people—volunteers from her campaign headquarters, clients with their legal problems. A long, busy day lay ahead of her.

Kathy prepared a cup of coffee, then sat, sipping it and gazing out her window, her back to her desk. She paid a high rent for this view—an extravagance that she did not regret. When the pressures piled up, she could take a moment now and then to look out at the open spaces, at the land that had nurtured her family for three generations, and she could think about her own ranch, the land that she had bought

with her own money, where she could escape on
weekends.

But now other thoughts occupied her mind. She
was still shaken by her encounter with Dak Roberts;
it was impossible to think about anything else.

The memories hurt. Seeing Dak this morning had
brought it all back sharp and clear. She achingly recalled how they had been high school sweethearts
here in Endless. They had been so much in love!
Even now, ten years later, she could still feel the tender, sweet awakening of first love. It had been a
stormy teenage romance; there had been lovers'
quarrels and tearful reconciliations. Dak had been
the jealous type; Kathy had had a mind of her own
and a hair-trigger temper. And they were both stubborn.

From her window she could see the courthouse
square in the center of downtown Endless. It was
here that Dak had given his speech after his triumphant Olympic win, bringing glory to himself and his
hometown. Along with the other citizens, Kathy's
heart had swelled with pride. For a change, their
town had become renowned for something besides its
humorous name while for Kathy, Dak's triumph had
a special, personal meaning.

But Dak's sweet triumph had turned bitter for
Kathy. The Olympic gold medal had opened doors

for Dak far beyond the wildest dreams of a small-town boy. He had followed his destiny, leaving his hometown behind and with it, Kathy's broken dreams.

They had both grown up in this coastal region with its rolling plains, chaparral-covered prairie and live oak trees tortured into grotesque shapes by the trade winds sweeping across the sand dunes. It was a semi-tropical region sometimes burned dry by long droughts and other times swept by flash floods that filled the dry creek beds called arroyos with raging torrents. The nights could be peaceful, the sky dotted with brilliant stars, the air cooled by breezes from the Gulf—breezes that could sometimes turn into raging hurricanes. It was a region of huge, sprawling ranches where oil was pumped from the earth while cattle grazed nearby and merchant ships sailed into the ports to load grain, cotton and wheat. Conquistadors had trod this land along with padres who had built missions now centuries old. Spanish was often heard more than English, a reminder that Mexico was less than a hundred and fifty miles to the west.

Kathy was reminded how deeply their lives had been shaped and molded by this land. Was that why Dak had come back?

Kathy closed her eyes, remembering the warm summers when Dak had worked at the community swimming pool as a lifeguard. Unlike Kathy, whose father owned one of the biggest ranches in the area, Dak lived on a modest farm a few miles from town. His parents struggled to barely make ends meet. Dak had welcomed the job both as a way of helping with his family's finances and the opportunity it gave him to spend hours every day perfecting his diving and swimming.

She recalled his easy gait as he strolled around the perimeter of the pool, his deep blue eyes squinting against the sun as he scanned the water.

That last summer she had spent a lot of time hanging around the pool even after it closed, helping him clean up and timing his laps as he practiced for the Olympics.

She knew he had an excellent chance of bringing home the gold medal. Having been trained by one of the best coaches, he'd already chalked up a long string of first-place trophies in national events.

In her mind's eye, she saw that summer through a golden haze—the picnics, the horseback rides, the movies where they held hands, the tender kisses that brought tears to her eyes and made her young body tremble with awakening hunger. Her eyes burned with tears now at those memories of moments gone forever.

Sometimes Kathy had swum with him. They even raced against each other. Of course she didn't stand a chance against him, but he gave her a large handicap to make it fun.

Had he ever been in love with her the way she had loved him? At the time she thought he had. But Dak's burning goal was to qualify for the Olympics; swimming was his ticket out of poverty. Nothing else was as important. They had shared those dreams, made plans for their exciting future when the fairy tale came true.

In the end, it came true for Dak, but not for her. Thinking about Dak's betrayal brought a wave of bitter regret.

Kathy's father had never approved of Dak; the matter had been a source of bitter family disputes. The mention of Dak Roberts's name to Burke Ayers was like a red flag waved at an angry bull, especially as Kathy spent more and more time with her steady boyfriend. "That Roberts kid is never going to amount to a hill of beans," Burke ranted. "Look at his father—a farmer working from sunup to sundown. Working that miserable, worn-out piece of land. You want to wind up married to a loser like that? You're not going steady with that boy and that's final!''

Burke's worst fear was that Kathy would do something foolish like run off with Dak and get married. The truth was that Kathy might have done just that, but Dak had better sense. "I love you, Kathy. I want the best for you. We'll get married when I can give it to you."

Burke Ayers was a big man—loud, forceful, domineering and by far the most powerful man in the community. In addition to ranching, he had numerous business interests in town, including Endless's bank where he was on the board of directors and owned a controlling interest in the stock. He was a man used to having his way. It was from him that Kathy had inherited a stubborn, determined streak, but as a teenager, she had not yet fully established her own identity. She lacked the self-assurance to assert her independence against her powerful father.

Dak had not liked Kathy's father any more than Burke liked him. A family feud between Dak's father and Burke Ayers went a long way back. Kathy didn't know the details, but whenever the subject of her father came up, Dak's lips thinned. He wouldn't talk about it, but let Kathy know he thought she let her father dominate her.

With a wrench of pain, she remembered the lovers' quarrel that had ended her high school romance with Dak. The next day, without even saying goodbye, Dak had taken a plane to California. For weeks, she waited and prayed for a letter from him—a letter that never came. The weeks became months. Eventually, Kathy heard that Dak had gotten married.

Dak Roberts had broken her heart; she would never forgive him for that. She had finally decided, regretfully, that her father had been right about Dak.

Burke Ayers had always been ambitious for her. She knew she would make him proud if she got a law degree and took over her grandfather's practice in Endless. She threw herself into her studies to forget about Dak. When she passed her bar exam, she came back home to open her law office. From a trust fund left her by her grandfather, she bought a small ranch a few miles from town and built a house. She had settled into the routine of her life here, enjoying her career and the outdoor life. She was involved in local civic affairs, having served two terms on the city council, and was now running for mayor. Her high school love affair with Dak Roberts had become a faded memory.

Suddenly, Dak had come back to Endless, back into her life, stirring up a storm of painful emotions. She hated him for breaking her heart. And yet, in spite of the hurt, was it possible the old chemistry was still there that could make her pulse leap at the sight of him? Ten years had put a few streaks of gray in his hair and etched faint lines around his eyes, but he still had the proud, erect bearing of an athlete. His waist was still trim, his shoulders square. He was mature now: a man had replaced the boy. His eyes were more sober, haunted perhaps by the tragic death of his wife and worry over his son's rebellious behavior. But that only added a deeper dimension to his character, made him even more attractive. A strange shiver ran through her.

Angry tears sprang to her eyes. "I wish you'd stayed in California, Dak Roberts!"

Chapter Two

Dak and his son were both silent on the ride back to the ranch. After Joedy's latest escapade, Dak's thoughts were in turmoil. Worry mingled with the emotional jolt of running into Kathy Ayers.

Lord, she looked good! he thought. Back in his high school she'd been the prettiest girl in the county. Now she was a woman, her body still slender, but rounded with maturity. She'd be in her late twenties, he realized, and she still didn't have a line in her face. Her hair was still as dark as night and her eyes were like large, deep black pools framed with sooty lashes. She had the healthy tan of a woman familiar with the outdoors. He remembered how much she loved horses; she probably spent a lot of time riding.

A fresh wave of old regret haunted him, the regret that he had ever left Endless ten years ago. With it came the anger at both Kathy and her father. Especially her father. It was that old despot who had come between them, who had set out to destroy Dak's father and then had virtually run Dak out of town. Thanks to Burke Ayers, nobody in Endless would give Dak a job. If Kathy had had the gumption to stand up to her old man maybe things would have turned out differently. But she'd been totally under his domination then and maybe she still was.

He remembered the feelings of regret when his marriage to Linda had become such a disappointment, the times he'd thought about how different his life might have been if he'd married Kathy instead of Linda.

Joedy was apparently thinking about Kathy, too. His young face was turned toward his father. "That was a nice lady," he said suddenly. "Who is she?"

"That's Miss Kathy Ayers, son."

Miss. Yes, she had not married; there had been no wedding ring on her finger. But he already knew that. People in a town the size of Endless had no secrets. When they were closing the deal on the ranch, old man Burkshire had brought him up to date on the status of Kathy Ayers along with the rest of the neighbors. "Willie Harkins owns the place west of you. You'll have trouble with Willie's bulls busting through the fence on your west pasture. You got to keep on him about that—make him pay for fixing it. To the south, you've got the highway to Brownsville and to the north the place goes as far as the railroad. On your east fence is Kathy Ayers's place." The grizzled old rancher gave him a sly look. "I reckon you know who she is. Seem to recollect you was sparkin' her back when the two of you was in high school, before you won that Olympic medal and went gallivantin' off to California. Miss Kathy's a lawyer now. Darn good one, too. I got her to make that blamed Willie Harkins pay me damages for his bulls bustin' down my fence. Folks here think a lot of Miss Ayers. They're runnin' her for mayor. Ain't that something? A woman mayor. Don't know what the world is coming to. In my day women stayed home where they belonged, but now they got this women's lib business, don't y' know."

Dak had felt a peculiar sensation warm his face when the garrulous old man had mentioned Kathy Ayers. What a strange twist of fate to make him Kathy's neighbor after all these years.

Resolutely, now, he put aside his thoughts about Kathy and turned his attention to a more pressing problem. "You had no business wandering off from the grocery store like that without telling me where you were going, Joedy. What gets into you to do things like that, anyway, son?"

Joedy shrugged. Dak saw the boy withdraw, just as he had when his mother had died. There was a wall around him that Dak couldn't break through.

"And that business about the aliens," Dak said gently. "Do you really believe there were aliens chasing you?"

Joedy just shrugged and looked away.

Dak sighed. No matter how hard he tried, he couldn't communicate with his son these days. He sometimes felt like a total failure as a father. Joedy had always been closer to Linda. Since his mother had been killed, Joedy had become a real discipline problem. He had become moody, rebellious, hard to control. He told lies, had nightmares, made up fantastic stories like the one he'd told Kathy. Several times he had run away.

Dak changed the subject. "Want to go for a ride when we get back to the ranch?"

The shadows in Joedy's eyes lightened. He looked around at Dak and nodded.

"I'll have Lefty saddle Stampede soon as we get back." Dak smiled. Of all the things he'd tried, buying Joedy the saddle horse had been the only thing that came close to helping Joedy over this rough time. Joedy loved the horse. Stampede was a small pinto, yellow, black and white. Junior Gomez, one of the hands on Dak's ranch, had been the cowboy who had originally broken the pinto to the saddle. A neighboring rancher had owned the horse and Junior had known he was for sale. "That's a gentle, steady little horse, good for a boy, Señor Dak," Junior had told him. "Horses got different personalities. Some are nervous, some are stupid, some are downright mean. But that Stampede is a calm, smart horse with a sweet disposition, and he's small. A good *caballo* for your boy, Joedy."

Dak had bought the horse that week. He decided it was worth every penny he paid for the pinto when he gave the reins to Joedy and saw a smile light his son's face for the first time in months.

Now Dak turned off the farm-to-market road onto a narrow, private lane that took them to the entrance of the ranch. The pickup truck rattled over a cattle guard. Above the entrance, *El Rancho Verde* was spelled out in metal letters, the ranch having been named after the lush vegetation fed by the winding creek across a prairie otherwise sparsely covered with cactus, mesquite and scrubby chaparral. The brand was a Circled "GR" for The Green Ranch.

When he bought the place from old Tod Burk-shire, who wanted to retire in the East where his daughter lived, Dak also acquired several ranch hands. There was Lefty Crawson, a venerable old cowhand with one eye blind as the result of a mule kick, an Adam's apple the size of a lemon that worked its way up and down in his stringy neck and skin as brown and leathery as his saddle. Despite his age, which must have been nearly seventy, and his constant grumbling about arthritis and other in-firmities, Lefty could work harder and longer than ranch hands half his years.

Junior Gomez, a twenty-year-old Mexican from Sonora who hoped to qualify as a citizen under the amnesty program, was good at breaking horses and also a willing worker, though lacking in Lefty's ex-perience.

Dak wasn't sure what to make of José Alemán, the mean-looking cook whose jagged scar down one cheek pulled the corner of his lip down in a perpet-ual scowl. His skin was swarthy, his eyebrows dark and heavy. In the evening he often sat on a stump behind the house and carved exquisite figures of horsemen out of pieces of wood. He would sit there for hours, shaving curly slivers of wood as thin as tissue paper with his razor-sharp knife. For no ap-parent reason, he would occasionally mutter something under his breath and hurl his knife with deadly accuracy at the side of the barn thirty feet away where it would stick, quivering in the fading light.

Junior Gomez told Dak that José Alemán had once been a chef in a big restaurant in Mexico City, but had gotten into some kind of trouble over a woman. Like Junior, he had crossed the Rio Grande late one night several years before. Dak was prepared for a steady diet of *enchiladas* and *juevos rancheros* and was pleasantly surprised to be served crisp salads, fresh vegetables, a variety of meats and desserts. After a few meals, Dak came to the conclusion that the story about José was true.

Dak was glad to keep the hands who kept the ranch running smoothly. Having grown up in South Texas on his parents' small farm, Dak was no greenhorn in the ranching business, and he knew that good workers meant fewer day-to-day problems. Lefty, Junior and José went about their jobs without requiring constant supervision. This place had been their home for several years and they treated it as such.

Making the move back to his hometown had been a big step, but Dak hoped the experience of healthy, outdoor ranch life would be good for Joedy and help him get over the loss of his mother.

Money was no longer Dak's problem; California had been good to him. He'd left Endless a poor boy but his fame had opened a lot of doors. TV commercials and promotions had earned him more money than he'd ever dreamed of having. Then he'd written a physical fitness guide that continued to sell well. He opened a health studio and sold franchises up and down the West Coast.

Yes, he'd made money—lots of it—but his personal life had been a disappointment. His marriage to Linda had been lukewarm. If they hadn't had Joedy, he was sure Linda would have left him. In the end, she had left. A tragic accident on a movie set had taken her life, leaving him with the difficult job of raising a son by himself.

So, life on the West Coast had lost its appeal to Dak. A part of him had always been homesick for Endless, and even though he'd grown up under tough circumstances, his roots were in Texas. He missed the long stretches of open prairie, the smell of wildflowers, the creak of saddle leather, the bright stars at night and the friendliness of the people.

Now he'd come back. Running into Kathy Ayers today gave him the strange feeling that he had stepped back into an unfinished chapter of a love story....

Chapter Three

Counselor, that was a very sneaky bit of court-room shenanigans,'' District Attorney Brice Williams remonstrated with mock severity.

Kathy grinned. "It won my client an acquittal."

They were having lunch in the Ramada Inn dining room on the interstate that skirted Endless. Brice had bet Kathy a lunch that the jury would send her client to jail. He had lost.

"Do you honestly think that Howard kid didn't swipe the TV set off the UPS delivery truck?" Brice asked, stirring a dollop of cream into his coffee.

Kathy shrugged. "The jury agreed with me, didn't they? You just didn't have much of a case, Brice.

One lousy witness. Old Mrs. Milton. The poor woman is hopelessly nearsighted.''

"I still think she recognized him," Brice grumbled.

"Reasonable doubt," Kathy reminded him. "Ah, here's lunch. That steak looks terrific."

"Enjoy," Brice said good-naturedly. "Any lawyer who runs a half dozen boys the same size and age as the accused, all dressed alike, past a nearsighted old lady in the witness stand and asks her to pick out a specific one deserves a steak. You had old lady Milton so rattled, she wouldn't have been able to identify King Kong!"

"You were objecting to every move I made," Kathy reminded him, "and Judge Davis overruled you."

"Yeah, and he could hardly keep from laughing. Anyway, enough shoptalk. Are you going to let me take you to the class reunion Friday night?"

The pleased glow on Kathy's face that had appeared after her victory now faded. She poked at her steak, wishing Brice hadn't reminded her of the class reunion.

"I—I don't know, Brice. I haven't made up my mind if I'm going."

"Undecided?" he exclaimed. "The tenth reunion of our graduation class of good old Endless High? Kathy, you can't miss that!"

"I know...." she murmured. *And Dak Roberts probably won't miss it, either,* she thought uncomfortably.

"I'm looking forward to it," Brice said with a grin. "It'll be great to see the old high school crowd, check out who married who, what couples have kids and where the waistlines are spreading and the hair receding."

Yes, she thought, it would be fun to see old classmates again. But what if Dak came? He probably would. After all, he had been in her graduating class, too. If he put in an appearance, there would be a lot of whispers and curious looks aimed her way. Everyone would remember their involvement. Theirs had been the big teenage-romance story of Endless High that year. All their friends had expected them to get married. The school crowd had been shocked when they broke up and Dak went off to California and married someone else. There had been all kinds of gossip at one time and now there would be a fresh wave of speculation. Kathy knew she would not only be painfully self-conscious, but confused and pain-filled at seeing Dak again.

If there were any way of skipping the reunion, she'd do it, but she couldn't very well pretend it wasn't taking place. She was chairman of the home-town planning committee that was putting on the event. She had accepted the job months ago before she knew Dak was moving back to Endless.

Brice was thinking the same thing. "I don't see how you can miss the reunion," he pointed out. "Everyone's depending on you to coordinate things."

"I know," she admitted. "By the way, are you going to come over to the gym tonight? You're on the decorating committee, you know."

"Oh, yeah. I'm supposed to bring the balloons, right?"

"Yes, and you promised to take care of the music."

"Got that taken care of. I booked Billy Jo's Wranglers. They play country and western for the kickers and rock for the rollers."

Kathy wasn't listening. She was lost in her own thoughts again as she looked at Brice, thinking how ironic it would be if she went to the reunion with Brice and Dak was there. It would be a replay right out of the past. Ten years before, the town had thrown a celebration party in Dak's honor when he won the Olympic gold medal. Her going to the party with Brice had precipitated the quarrel that broke them up and sent Dak off to California without saying goodbye.

The whole thing had been so senseless. She had never cared for Brice other than as a friend; her father had made that she go to the party with Brice that night. Later when Dak didn't write or call, she had run around with Brice to keep from feeling lonely. Brice gave her an engagement ring and all their friends assumed they'd marry. Eventually, though, she knew it was impossible. Dak had spoiled her for anyone else. With Dak Roberts she had known true love. Until she could feel that way about someone again, she preferred to remain single. So, she gave Brice back his engagement ring and went off to law school. Brice, too, chose to pursue a legal career. Or maybe he just went to the same school hoping Kathy would change her mind about him.

Now when she looked at Brice she saw a well-fed, well-dressed man who exuded success and self-confidence. Brice came from one of the leading ranching families in the area. His father and Kathy's father were business associates and life-long friends. Burke Ayers made no bones about the fact that he wished Kathy would get some sense in her stubborn head and marry Brice. His grandchildren, Burke Ayers grumbled, were long overdue.

Brice had held the job of district attorney for the past four years. It was generally accepted that he would soon be moving up the political ladder to run for state representative. Actually, the two of them had much in common. They had remained good friends, dating occasionally. Brice hadn't married, and he'd made it clear that he still had the engagement ring; but marriage was not something she wanted to deal with now.

"Brice, thanks for the lunch. I have to get back to my office."

"You hardly ate."

"Guess I wasn't as hungry as I thought."

Brice took care of the check and they headed out to the parking lot. "How's the mayor's race going?" he asked casually.

"It isn't a race yet," she reminded him. "We're just setting up the campaign. There's still several weeks before the end of the filing deadline and we're not sure who we might be up against."

"I don't think anybody else is going to run. You'll just have to beat the incumbent, old man Jimpson, and you shouldn't have any trouble doing that. He's been mayor of Endless since the Great Flood. The citizens want a change."

"Yeah, but a woman mayor? Brice, this is a very conservative, western constituency. There's still considerable hangover of frontier mores. Some of the crusty old ranchers around here may take a dim view of a woman running their town. Their idea of women's lib is to buy the little woman a washing machine to replace her washboard."

Brice laughed. "Come on, Kathy. You're exaggerating. Endless isn't that far behind the times...."

Kathy struggled all week with the decision of whether or not to go to the class reunion. As chairman of the reunion committee, she was so involved with the planning that it became increasingly obvious there was no way she could gracefully stay home. One last-minute crisis after another kept her racing all Friday afternoon.

Finally she was able to go home to take a shower. She was undecided about what to wear. People were informal in Endless. Some of the men would show up at the reunion in sports coats. Others, like Brice, would wear suits. The women would probably be more dressy, though no one would wear a cocktail dress. Tonight, Kathy felt she needed a touch of sophistication to bolster her morale. She decided on a two-piece blue-and-white plaid silk dress with a blue belt. It had short sleeves, a tight bodice and a straight skirt with a slit in back.

Kathy was slightly breathless but ready when Brice parked in her driveway shortly after dusk.

"You look gorgeous," he observed after they were in his car, headed into town. "As usual."

"I feel like a wreck. Remind me never to be the chairman of a reunion committee again."

"Last-minute problems?"

"One after another. You remember the Pattersons agreed to barbecue a side of beef? We were going to serve barbecue, pinto beans and salad. Martha Patterson called me early this afternoon—Jim had some kind of accident with his hay bailer and broke his arm. I had to find a caterer out of Kingsville who agreed to deliver the entire barbecue. Then we discovered the air conditioner in the gym had conked out. Then at five o'clock, Mrs. Anderson called to say she had an allergy attack and couldn't make the welcoming address."

Brice chuckled. "Mrs. Anderson and her allergies. I remember her sniffing us all the way through English 102. Who's taking her place?"

"Coach Wilkins."

Brice winced. "We'll get a rambling discourse on every football game Endless High ever won."

"Well, it was the best I could do on such short notice," Kathy replied testily.

By the time they got to the high school gym, some of their old classmates had already arrived. There was a flurry of greetings, hugs and handshakes.

Kathy hurried around, checking to see that the name tags were near the entrance, conferring with the caterers, coping with a few minor problems such as the placement of the portable bar and locating electrical outlets for the band's amplifiers.

Class reunions, Kathy thought, could be emotionally wrenching affairs. True, it was fun to see old classmates again, but the meetings were a reminder of a youth now gone forever. Some graduates had never left and Kathy was used to seeing them. It was the ones who had moved away after graduation who put a clear perspective on the change of time. Gone were the football heroes, the cheerleaders, the honor roll students and the class clowns. Gone was the painful self-consciousness, the shyness, the false bravado of teenagers. Now the boys were men talking about their jobs and the girls had become women exchanging experiences in juggling careers with homemaking and motherhood.

Kathy relaxed as the reception and cocktail hour got underway. The air conditioner purred smoothly; the caterers ran the portable bar efficiently; the band, which would get loud later, kept their amplifiers turned down so people could talk; the gym looked festive with clusters of balloons and streamers in the school colors of gold and white.

In the excitement, Kathy had temporarily pushed thoughts of Dak Roberts to the background. Then she noticed a group clustered around a late arrival. "Hey, look—it's Dak Roberts!" she heard someone exclaim.

Yes, there he was—broad-shouldered, handsome in a white sport jacket that emphasized his deep tan, taller than most of the other men.

She turned her back, escaped to the bar and stood there trembling, concentrating on watching the bartender pour her a fresh drink. Out of the corner of her eye, just as she'd expected, she saw some of the crowd looking at her curiously. Suddenly the air conditioner no longer seemed to be doing its job. Her face felt hot.

It was time for the banquet and everyone took seats at rows of long tables. Kathy found a place as far away from Dak Roberts as possible.

Bill Sawyer, who had been senior-class president, gave the invocation. Coach Wilkins made the welcoming address, a rambling series of sports anecdotes that had nothing whatsoever to do with anyone present. The dinner was served. Kathy poked at the food on her plate and talked with Martha Dickerson on her left, who could never get a date in high school and now had five kids, the youngest a set of twins, and Vernon Stutler on her right, who had flunked bookkeeping their senior year and had since become a successful car dealer in San Antonio.

After the meal, the band turned up their amplifiers. Vernon Stutler asked Kathy to dance. After that she danced with Billy Sawyer and then with Brice. She was just beginning to entertain a glimmer of confidence that she might survive the evening when Dak Roberts strolled up and asked her for a dance.

Kathy's mind momentarily went blank. Her instinct of self-preservation almost made her turn away, but people were staring at them. She stood there feeling helpless as Dak took her in his arms. The band was playing a slow, sad country and western song about a love gone wrong. *How fitting,* she thought desperately.

Dak swept her across the floor. She'd forgotten how strong his arms really were. She'd forgotten how well they danced together.

Her heart was pounding. The closeness of their bodies made her blood run hot. Despite all that had happened, despite her anger and bitterness, the chemistry was still there; the physical attraction still smoldered. She felt embarrassed that she could allow herself to become so aroused over a man who had walked out on her. And yet, held in the warm circle of Dak's arms, their bodies touching, Kathy had the strange, dreamy sensation that they were floating on air. Far above the old school. It seemed as though the hands of time had moved backward and this was their high school prom. Memories of other times and other places brought a lump to her throat and a mist to her eyes—the almost unbearable sweetness of Dak's first kiss, the private little jokes they laughed about, the walks in the moonlight, the dreams they shared, the touch of Dak's hand, the special look in his eyes that shut out the world and placed her at the center of his universe. How could it have ended?

Dak had left. She came back to the present with a fresh rush of anger.

"I see you haven't forgotten how to dance," Dak said.

She didn't reply.

"We were always good together on the dance floor, weren't we, Kathy? Remember the senior prom?"

She thought about the faded, dry corsage crumbling to dust in a box of memorabilia in her closet. Angrily she wondered why she hadn't thrown it away years before. She'd do it as soon as she got home!

Dak was looking down at her with an expression she couldn't interpret. Then a smile tugged at his lips.

"Do you still have a lousy temper?" he teased. "As I remember, that was what broke us up."

"It was not," she said furiously. "It was your jealous streak. You found out I was going with Brice Williams to that dance given in your honor after your Olympic win and you took off for California without even saying goodbye."

"I heard you didn't lose any time getting engaged to Brice," Dak said coldly.

"Well, I was mad and hurt. I wanted to get back at you. But I didn't marry Brice. Anyway, what difference did it make? You forgot about me once you were in California. You married someone else. You didn't write me even one letter."

"Of course I wrote. Several times. You never answered."

Kathy frowned, stunned. "Are—are you telling me the truth about the letters?" she asked in an unsteady voice. A letter from Dak could have made all the difference.

"Certainly I'm telling the truth. Why would I lie?"

"I don't know. I don't even know why you had the nerve to ask me to dance! But I never got any letters from you. I swear it."

He frowned, giving her a troubled, angry, searching look. "Now it's my turn to ask if you're telling the truth."

"I don't have any more reason to lie than you do. But what could have happened to the letters?"

Dak's face darkened. "I wouldn't put it past your father to have intercepted them. He wanted to break us up, you know. He as good as ran me out of town. I bet Burke Ayers was delighted when I left for California."

"Daddy wouldn't have done a thing like that," she said, but not with complete conviction. It was true that her father had been dead set against her getting serious over Dak. And Burke Ayers was a big, forceful man who was used to ordering people around and getting his way.

"You always were daddy's little girl," Dak said bitterly. "You never had a mind of your own where your father was concerned. You didn't have the gumption to stand up to him. I hear you're running for mayor of Endless. You shouldn't have a bit of trouble getting elected. Big daddy Burke Ayers will buy the election for his precious little girl!"

Kathy's black eyes blazed with anger. "Dak Roberts, how dare you talk like that."

Dak looked down at her with his strange, crooked smile. "I'll dare. But it won't do any good. I never could talk to you about your daddy. Well, lucky for me he's not here tonight. At least I got one chance to remember what a little ball of fire you are.''

With a low chuckle that infuriated her even more, he turned and walked away, leaving her standing on the dance floor, seething.

Chapter Four

The angry confrontation with Dak left Kathy profoundly shaken. She left the reunion that night with a blinding headache and spent a miserable night, tossing and turning. The next morning, she decided to pay her father a visit.

Her emotions were ranging from cold fury at Dak to a feeling of uncertainty. What if Dak were telling the truth about the letters?

The awful things he'd said about her father had infuriated her. His accusations of her lacking the backbone to stand up to her father and, not having a mind of her own made her even madder.

Suddenly she became uncomfortable when she thought back to the unforgettable fight that had broken her and Dak up. Dak had come back an Olympic winner, the town hero. There'd been a parade and speeches in his honor, and then a dance was given in his benefit. Naturally, he'd wanted Kathy at his side, but her father had put his foot down. "You're not going to that dance with Dak Roberts and that's final," her father told her. "You can go with Brice Williams or you can stay home."

Brice's father was the owner of one of the largest ranches in the area, and was a longtime friend of Kathy's dad. It was no secret that a marriage between the offspring would benefit both families.

Remembering how she'd caved in that time made her flush uncomfortably. She hated to admit it, but it was about as easy to stand up to the overpowering personality of Burke Ayers as it was to stop a freight train with a tennis racquet.

He and her mother had separated when Kathy was an infant. Her mother died when she was six and she returned to the ranch where she'd been born to be raised by her father. It seemed, to a little girl growing up, that the big man was always in command of every situation, always right. She did let him make decisions for her.

All that changed after she went to college. She declared her independence. From the trust set up by her grandfather, she was able to buy her own place and get out from under the dominating shadow of her father. By then she had seen that Burke Ayers's bark was a lot worse than his bite. Under his gruff exterior there was a deep love for her. He had only wanted what he thought best for her. They remained good friends and she loved him as much as ever, but she let him know that she was now a woman running her own life, a fact that Burke had, in time, grudgingly accepted, though he continued to offer unsolicited advice on everything from how to run her ranch to her law practice—advice that went in one ear and out the other.

His ranch, which had been her home until she got her own place, was a half hour's drive away. Her car sped down the rural routes that had once been dirt country lanes that turned into muddy quagmires when it rained. Now they were paved farm-to-market roads.

When she parked in the driveway near the sprawling white stucco ranch house, she heard her father's voice coming from the direction of the corrals. He had a resonant baritone that could be heard a quarter of a mile away.

Kathy walked around the house and found him astride a big, restless quarter horse, shouting orders to some hands herding cattle into a corral chute. Burke Ayers was in his sixties now. His hair had turned snow white and he had a touch of arthritis in his hands that played havoc with his roping, but he was as active as ever. His bearing was soldier straight, a carryover from his days in the military.

When he'd been a teenager, Burke had gotten into a row with his father and gone off to join the army. He had been in the thick of fighting in Korea. About the time that was over, his father had a stroke and Burke came back to take over operations of the ranch that had been in the family since trail-herding days. He'd been a rancher ever since. He'd married late, having Kathy when he was nearly forty. Kathy could remember little about his relationship with her mother and Burke refused to talk about it. She assumed they had not gotten along because they split up when Kathy was very young.

He caught sight of her now as she waved, and he wheeled his horse around, trotted up to the ranch house and swung out of the saddle. The quarter horse tossed his head angrily and tried to pull away, but Burke kept a firm grip on the reins. He called to one of his hands to come get the animal.

"That's a mean-looking brute," Kathy said, giving the horse a critical look.

"Tell me about it," Burke muttered. "Last week he bit me. I was about ready to shoot him, but he's the best cutting horse I've got."

"I wish you wouldn't ride horses like that, Daddy," she said with a worried expression. "You're going to get thrown and hurt."

"That'll be the day," he grunted. "Come on in. I'll buy you a drink."

"This early in the morning? It'll have to be coffee."

"That's what I mean." He chuckled to himself as he strode onto the front porch.

"Yeah, I know how you drink your coffee—with bourbon instead of cream!"

His boots rang on the gleaming Mexican tile of the big, main room of the ranch house. The housekeeper served them coffee. Burke sat in an easy chair, propping his boots on the rugged, heavy oak coffee table.

"How's the campaign shaping up?" he asked gruffly.

She looked at him with surprise. Had he read her mind? With Dak's angry accusations still ringing in her ears, she'd come out here to get the whole story from her dad. She knew he swung a lot of political clout in this area. Most of the old-time ranchers and business people were his lifelong cronies and he had been on the board of directors of the town bank since before Kathy was born. No doubt he could have a lot of influence on the mayoral election. It was the last thing she wanted. If she got elected it was going to be on her own, not because she was Burke Ayers's daughter. She had come here to tell him that if he had any ideas about sticking his foot into the campaign, to forget it, but she didn't want to launch into that matter immediately. There were other things bothering her. She wanted to talk about them, but wasn't sure how to begin.

She sipped her coffee, making small talk about people they both knew. Then in a casual voice, she said, "Did you know Dak Roberts had moved back here?"

She saw a dark shadow pass over Burke's face. "Yeah, I heard," he muttered.

"You never did like him, did you, Daddy? I remember you kept trying to break us up."

Burke shrugged. He refilled his coffee cup and splashed a generous dollop of sour-mash bourbon in the steaming black liquid. "I didn't think he was good enough for you. His daddy never amounted to a hill of beans. You know the old saying, 'the chips don't fall far from the tree.' All Dak did was spend his time hanging around the swimming pool.''

"He was in training for the Olympics. He won a gold medal, you know.''

"Yeah, I know.'' Burke gave her a piercing look, his dark eyes speculative under shaggy white eyebrows. "You still got a thing for him?''

Kathy felt her face grow hot and busily poured a second cup of coffee, angry with the way her fingers fumbled. "Oh, of course not, Daddy. That was a long time ago. We were teenagers.''

She looked up at her father, burning to question him about Dak's letters, but realized the futility. If he had intercepted them, he wouldn't admit it. "Y'know," she began slowly, "I've sometimes wondered why you disliked Dak and his family so much. It seemed to be more than just the fact that they were poor. I get the impression that Dak Roberts has a lot of hostility toward you, too. Was there some kind of family feud I didn't know about?''

His eyes darkened for a moment. Then he scowled and the strange black glitter was gone. He shrugged. "I just didn't think the boy was good enough for you," he muttered. "I wanted you to make something of your life—go on to college and be somebody. I was afraid you'd wind up in a teenage marriage to the Roberts kid and mess up your life."

The explanation didn't completely satisfy Kathy, but she didn't press the issue. She knew her father well enough to know when he'd closed a subject.

"Speaking of marriage," her father said, "are you and Brice ever going to tie the knot? You've kept that boy dangling for years. He's not going to wait around forever, y'know."

"Dad!" she remonstrated. "You promised to butt out of my love life, remember?"

"Well I'd like to have some grandchildren before I'm in a nursing home!" he grumbled.

She changed the subject abruptly. "Speaking of butting out," she began with mock severity, "I want a word with you about the mayoral race."

"What about it?"

"Well, I know how you just love local politics. You aren't by any chance thinking of twisting a few arms to get me elected, are you?"

He stared at her. "What gave you that notion?"

"Don't look so innocent, Daddy. I know how many cronies you have around here. Burke Ayers happens to be a pretty powerful man in these parts. If he made up his mind to get his daughter elected mayor, not much could stop her."

"What's so bad about a little help? You want the office, don't you?"

"Yes, but I want to win this election on my own merit. I want to win because people think I'm best qualified for the job, not because I'm Burke Ayers's daughter."

Her father gave her a long, hard look. When she was a child, that look had been enough to make her knees quiver. Now she just raised her chin and glared back at him.

His response was a low, deep chuckle. "Somewhere along the line you sure sprouted a mind of your own. Okay, go run your own race. But I hope you don't mind if I vote for you."

She laughed and gave him an impulsive hug. "You know how much I love you, don't you?"

For the next several days, Kathy was in court litigating a civil case. She planned to relax over the weekend and tend to a few chores around her ranch. But Dak Roberts's unexpected appearance interrupted the peace and quiet of the Texas prairie.

Kathy's ranch, the Lazy K, was a modest spread compared to the big, productive cattle operations in the area. She was like many South Texas professionals who owned farms and ranches as a sideline. She ran a small herd of Santa Gertrudis cattle that she'd bought from the King ranch, but the livestock did little more than pay for the ranch's basic expenses.

Kathy knew the cattle business as well as she knew her law practice. She could rope calves, doctor cows, repair fences and brand as efficiently as any rancher in the area, but she couldn't run the place single-handedly. Beto Garza, his wife, Maria, and their six children lived in a tenant house on the ranch. Beto took care of the heavy chores and Maria kept the ranch house spotless and prepared meals for Kathy when she was too busy to cook for herself.

When Kathy had bought the place, the main ranch house was in disrepair. She had had it completely re-modeled. It was a long, rambling structure with thick walls, Mexican tile floors, spacious rooms and heavy beamed ceilings—pure Spanish mission architecture. Kathy loved it. The house was her refuge from the pressures of her career and twentieth-century life. Out here, miles from city lights and traffic, the stars were so hot and bright it seemed she could reach up and pluck them from the dark velvet night. She was lulled to sleep by the medley of the cicada's whine in the mesquite trees, the rustle of jack rabbits scurrying through the brush, the nicker of a restless horse in the corral and the croak of a bullfrog at the watering tank. In the mornings, she could eat breakfast on the screened porch and watch deer graze in the dewy grass of the ranch yard.

Sometimes she entertained friends from town, filling the big rooms with guests, holding fiestas in the yard where jack-o'-lanterns were strung between the trees, Mariachis strummed their guitars and the aroma of mesquite smoke wafted from the pit where Beto barbecued beef and *cabrito*.

It was on Saturday, a week after the reunion, that Kathy was having a late breakfast on her screened porch when she saw a rider coming across the prairie toward her house. At first he was no more than a speck in the distance, coming from the west. Her curiosity was aroused and she settled down to sip her coffee and wait as she watched the rider draw nearer.

Gradually, Kathy could identify a small cow pony—yellow, black and white—the kind of horse called a pinto or calico. The rider was quite small, possibly a woman.

Soon the horse and rider were close enough for Kathy to see clearly that the rider was a young boy. And when he rode into her yard, she saw it was Dak's son, Joedy.

With a mixture of feelings, primarily surprise, Kathy put down her coffee and opened the screen door. She walked across the yard to where Joedy had stopped. He was sitting on his horse, looking around uncertainly.

"Good morning, Joedy," Kathy said.

Joedy nervously fiddled with his reins. His horse flicked his tail, shook his head restlessly, then moved a few steps to an appetizing clump of grass.

"You're quite a way from home," Kathy observed.

The boy shrugged.

Kathy gave him a thoughtful look, then smiled and patted his horse. "Good-looking cow pony. What's his name?"

"Stampede."

Kathy laughed. "Stampede? He looks tamer than that. Hey, why don't you get down and come over to the porch? I was just having breakfast. What would you say to some cinnamon rolls and milk?"

Joedy nodded. "Okay."

"Tell you what. I bet Stampede would like some breakfast, too. Let's lead him over to the corral and I'll give him a bucket of oats. Okay?"

"Yes, ma'am."

"My, you're a polite boy. Not many kids say 'Ma'am' these days."

When they were seated at the porch table, Kathy watched Joedy wolf down a pile of cinnamon rolls and several glasses of milk. "You must have been starved. Didn't you have any breakfast?"

Joedy shook his head.

"You rode all the way from your daddy's ranch. You must have left about sunup. Guess you didn't have time for breakfast. What made you decide to go for such a long ride?"

The boy stared down at his plate, blushing. "I was hoping you'd come over to see me so I could show you my horse. When you didn't come, I decided to come see you."

"I see," Kathy murmured, nodding slowly. "How did you know where I lived, Joedy?"

"I heard my father and Lefty—he's our foreman—talk about the people who live around here. They said your place was next to ours over in this direction. I figured if I rode this way long enough I'd see your house."

"Well, I'm glad you came to visit me, Joedy, but you could have gotten lost."

"Oh, I didn't have any trouble about that except when the Indians almost caught me."

Kathy kept her face grave. "So the Indians chased you, did they?"

"Um-hmm. A whole bunch of them. They was gonna scalp me, but Stampede outran them."

"Good thing you have a fast horse."

"Sure is."

He was overcoming his initial shyness. Looking straight at her now, his face was animated as he talked.

"Are you still hungry?"

"A little bit."

"How would you like a bowl of fresh strawberries with whipped cream?"

He relaxed enough to smile. "That sounds good."

"Okay. You stay here now and have some more milk. I'll go get the strawberries."

Kathy went into her bedroom, far enough from the porch so Joedy couldn't hear her. She picked up the phone. After their confrontation at the reunion, the last thing she wanted to do was talk to Dak Roberts, but it was obvious Joedy had undertaken this ride without permission and she had a runaway boy on her hands. She got Dak's number from information and she made her fingers push the numbers as she braced herself for the sound of Dak's voice. When it came over the wire, she drew a breath and forced an impersonal tone into her voice. "This is Kathy Ayers."

There was a surprised silence.

She quickly added, "Your son paid me a visit this morning."

A soft gasp sounded over the line. "He's with you? Thank God! We have been out looking everywhere for that boy."

There was no mistaking the tension and worry in his voice. Her anger softened. No matter how furious he had made her, he was at the moment a distraught parent. She had to feel a measure of compassion.

"I'll come right over and get him," Dak said.

"All right. No—wait a minute. You're mad and you're going to take it out on Joedy. Maybe you'd better wait until you cool down a bit."

"I've been too easy on him," Dak growled. "I think the time has come to give him a good talking-to. He could have gotten lost or seriously hurt, riding out onto the prairie alone like that."

"Well, he's your son."

"That sounds like a polite way of telling me reprimanding isn't the answer."

Kathy didn't answer. She had no intention of getting into a debate over child rearing with a parent as distraught as Dak. Instead, she asked, "What d'you suppose got into him to come all the way over here?"

Dak was silent for a moment, then said slowly, "I told you, Joedy's been going through a real bad time since his mother died. I think he took a shine to you the other day when you bought him that ice cream.

He's mentioned you several times, saying he wished you'd come see him. I'm just guessing—I'm certainly no psychologist—but maybe you fill a need he has right now, a kind of mother substitute.''

Kathy thought that over. "How would it be if you let him visit me for a few hours? I don't have anything planned this morning. After lunch, I'll saddle a horse and ride with him back to your place.''

There was a note of surprise in Dak's reply. "That's—darn nice of you, Kathy. But I don't want to impose...."

The anger in his voice was missing now. Her own harsh feelings softened, submerged by a wave of sympathy. The problems Dak was facing, trying to be both a father and mother to his boy, were staggering. The note of worry in his voice was unmistakable.

"It's no imposition,'' she said quickly. "I like Joedy. We hit it off fine. He'll be good company. I'll put him to work helping me with some chores around the place this morning and I'll see he's back home by midafternoon.''

"All right. I know Joedy will be in seventh heaven.'' Dak hesitated, then added, "Thank you, Kathy,'' and hung up.

She saw a remarkable transformation in Joedy as the morning progressed. The sad, withdrawn look in his eyes faded. His shyness and reserve melted. Soon he was chattering away, completely at ease with her. He went about the chores energetically. They cleaned out a hayloft, doctored a sick calf, weeded her garden and painted a gate. He had a healthy appetite for lunch. In the afternoon, Kathy saddled her favorite horse, an Appaloosa mare.

"Gee that's a pretty saddle," Joedy said, looking enviously at Kathy's ornate, hand-tooled leather.

"Thanks, Joedy. My father gave it to me for my birthday last year. He had it handmade in Mexico."

When they rode into the yard at the main house on Dak's ranch, the place seemed deserted. Then they circled the house to where the barn and corrals were located and a surprising sight met Kathy's eyes.

Dak had had an Olympic-size swimming pool installed in the spacious backyard. Kathy pulled her reins, stopping her horse. She sat there motionless, her eyes drawn to the sight of Dak Roberts poised on the diving board, his body gleaming like a magnificent bronze statue in the sunlight. He was taking controlled breaths, so deep in concentration he hadn't noticed them. Then he sprang from the board and entered the water in a dive so perfectly executed it took Kathy's breath away.

Once again she experienced that strange momentary déjà vu; she was a teenager again, in love with watching her hero practicing for the Olympics. She quickly recovered herself.

Dak crossed the pool in powerful strokes and clambered out. He spotted them and hurried across the turf in long strides. Drops of water glistened on his smooth, tanned skin like diamonds in the bright Texas sunlight. Kathy saw how his brief swimming trunks hugged his firm hips, how fit and hard his nearly nude physique was, muscles rippling, shoulders broad and strong. He was like a powerful jungle cat loping toward them. As he drew closer, she was acutely aware of his body in an intimate way that brought waves of heat radiating to her flesh and made her heart quicken. She couldn't pull her gaze away from him.

At first his gaze was directed toward his son, but then he looked at Kathy. For a moment their eyes met. A tremor coursed through her leaving her weak.

Chapter Five

The momentary spell was broken when Dak turned his full attention toward his son and Kathy was relieved to see that Dak had calmed down since their telephone conversation. He gave Joedy a stern lecture about the dangers of riding across the prairie alone, and afterward tousled his boy's sandy hair.

Having delivered Joedy safely, Kathy was about to rein her horse around and return home, but Dak quickly moved around Joedy's horse to her side. "Kathy...thank you. I know Joedy had a great time at your place today. I want you to know how much I appreciate what you did for him."

"It's okay," she said stiffly. "I enjoyed it as much as he did."

She started to pull away, but Dak reached up and grabbed her reins. "Could you stay for a while?"

"I—I need to get home...."

"Just a minute, please." He turned to his son. "Joedy, ride over to the corral and get Lefty to help you unsaddle your horse, okay?"

The boy nodded, but didn't move immediately. His eyes were pleading with Kathy. "Dad, could she eat supper with us?"

Dak nodded in agreement. "Sounds like a good idea, son."

He looked at Kathy for a reply. But she kept her eyes away from him, directing a smile at the boy. "Maybe another time, Joedy...."

"But—"

"Son, go do what I said," Dak reminded him firmly.

"Aw, gee..." Appearing to be on the verge of tears, Joedy reluctantly nudged his horse and headed in the direction of the corrals.

"Looks like you've made a conquest," Dak said to Kathy, adding, "I was hoping you could stay a while. Maybe we could go for a ride and I could show you around, then you could have supper with us." While his eyes weren't begging with her to stay as

Joedy's had, there was a soft sincerity in them that she remembered all too well from the old days. "I'd like to talk to you about Joedy."

Suddenly, she swung down from her saddle and stood facing Dak, her eyes blazing. "Why the sudden burst of hospitality? At the reunion the other night you were treating me like a case of food poisoning."

"I had a few things to get off my chest," he said abruptly.

"Such as?"

"Just as I told you. I thought I got a raw deal from you ten years ago."

"I thought the same!" she said hotly.

Dak's anger had returned full force. "Maybe your father did intercept my letters. Still, he wouldn't have had so much control over your life if you hadn't let him."

"Dak, I was a teenager living at home. I had to do what my father told me to do."

Dak nodded. With sharp irony in his voice, he said, "A lot of people in Endless do what your father tells them to do. Ten years ago, he made certain none of the people in this town would give me a job."

"I find that hard to believe."

"Well, it's true."

"If it is true, then he did you a favor. You went on to California and obviously did all right for yourself. What kind of future would you have had in Endless?"

"You have a point," he agreed. "I guess that's one thing I can thank Burke Ayers for—the only thing. Not that he thought he was helping me or anybody in my family out."

Kathy gave him a penetrating look. "Just what is this feud between you and my father, anyway? I have the feeling it goes a lot deeper than just his trying to come between us. Something happened that turned him against you and your family. What was it?"

Dak shrugged. "Why don't you ask him about it?"

"I did. He won't give me a straight answer, either."

Dak sighed. "Kathy, this isn't getting us anywhere. We're just tearing ourselves up. Why don't we sign a truce for today? Time out. I'd really like to talk to you about Joedy. I think you may have a key to what's troubling him. When he's around you he seems to be happier and more his old self than I've seen him in the past year. It would mean a lot to him if you'd have supper with us."

And what would it mean to you, Dak Roberts? she wondered.

"If you can't stay for supper," he went on when Kathy didn't respond to his invitation, "at least go for a ride with me so we can have a talk about Joedy."

His direct, hypnotic gaze held her captive. She felt as if she were drowning in the depths of his intense blue eyes and hated herself for the weakness. Her better judgment warned her that spending any more time around Dak was only going to acerbate a lot of old painful emotional wounds. But where Dak was concerned she had never acted rationally.

"All right," she agreed reluctantly. "Just a short ride though and then I'm going home."

Dak nodded, looking at her gravely. For a moment they were facing one another. She could almost feel the heat of his body...his magnificent body, bare and temptingly close. Again she felt a familiar tremble ripple through her. A warm sensation suffused her body—her thighs, her arms, her lips. Her breasts swelled with a longing for his touch.

"Why don't you come in the house and have something cool to drink while I change?"

With a determined effort, she shook off the spell that Dak's closeness had cast over her. "Thanks," she said coolly, "but I think I'll wait over at the corral with Joedy."

She led her horse over to the fence, wrapped her reins around a post and clambered up to the top rail. Joedy, having taken care of his horse, ran over and climbed up beside her. "Are you going to stay?" he asked, his eyes bright with excitement.

"For a little while, Joedy. Your dad talked me into going for a ride so he could show me around your ranch."

Joedy's face fell. "I was hoping you could come up and see my room. I've got a lot of neat computer games and—"

She smiled. "Well, I'd like to, Joedy, but I already promised your dad I'd go for a ride with him."

"Maybe when you get back, then?"

"Well . . . maybe," she said, "but I can't promise. It'll be getting late and I need to get home."

"You could stay for supper," he suggested hopefully.

"Better not count on that, Joedy."

Dak, dressed in jeans, a shirt and a pair of scuffed-up boots, came out of the house and walked up to where they were sitting. "Ready for that ride?"

She nodded.

"Can I go, too?" Joedy asked.

"Not this time, son," Dak smiled. "You've had Miss Ayers to yourself all day. You go on in and take a shower. Looks like you need one pretty bad."

Joedy sighed, but with a look of resignation, he turned and headed toward the house.

In the corral, Dak tossed a saddle onto a big bay mare, pulled the cinch tight and swung into the saddle in one smooth move. It was easy to see that he was as at home on a horse as he was in a swimming pool.

He called to Lefty Crawson to open the corral gate, and rode around to where Kathy had mounted her own horse.

Kathy was silent as they rode out of the ranch yard. She felt self-conscious and awkward. Dak appeared to be content to keep his thoughts to himself, too. She followed his lead in a westerly direction, riding across a wide expanse of grazing land covered with brush and scrubby chaparral. Presently they came to a wooded area. The ground sloped down to a creek bed where a clear mountain stream bubbled over a graveled bed.

They stopped at the edge of the creek while the horses drank.

Dak's gaze was drawn to Kathy. She looked lovely... and all too desirable. She was slightly disheveled from the ride. Her hair hung loose and tousled, framing the perfect oval of her face. Her skin gleamed with the faint sheen of perspiration. His gaze trailed down to the hollow of her throat and the hint of a soft, shadowy valley where the top button of her shirt was open. Her full, rounded breasts strained against the shirt with each breath. Her jeans tightly outlined her thighs as she sat astride her horse.

A surge of desire caught him by surprise. He was acutely aware of her, aware of their isolation here on the prairie.

He had convinced himself he was completely over Kathy Ayers. She was a chapter out of his past. He'd wanted nothing more to do with her, or her father. Now he wasn't so sure. At that moment he wanted her, wanted to take her in his arms, to kiss her, to unbutton her blouse, to bury his face in her soft, yielding secrets, to satisfy what had been denied him ten years ago.

He regained his sanity with an effort, reining in his runaway desire as he would a bucking bronco. He reminded himself of where his desire for Kathy had gotten him ten years ago. Had anything really changed? Kathy appeared to have matured, to be more sure of herself, more independent. But looks could be deceiving. The specter of Burke Ayers came between them, making him cautious.

"This is a lovely spot," Kathy said, her voice impersonal as she looked around at the pecan and oak trees that shaded the grassy oasis.

Dak nodded. "I looked at several ranches in the area. There were some I could have gotten a better deal on, but this creek sold me on buying this place from Tod Burkshire."

"I envy you the running water. On my place, I had a bulldozer dig a watering tank that has turned into something of a man-made lake. But there's nothing like having a natural stream on your land."

"Well, there are all kinds of legends about Indians camping on this creek. Might be true. Joedy found several arrowheads—excited him no end."

Kathy smiled. "He thinks the Indians are still around. Do you know some braves on the warpath chased him on his way to my place this morning?"

Dak looked troubled. "Another one of his wild stories. The boy lives in a world of fantasy. His little escapade this morning is a real good example. D'you think I should take him to a child psychiatrist?"

Kathy shifted in her saddle uncomfortably. "I'm no expert on children, Dak."

"But you spent most of today with him. You must have formed some opinion about him."

"He seemed pretty normal to me, once he got over his initial shyness."

Dak nodded slowly. "I think you're able to draw him out of his shell, out of the fantasy world he lives in."

"Maybe he found out the real world is too painful. The real world took his mother away. He just needs time for the hurt to go away or at least become less painful."

Dak sighed. "I hope you're right."

He prodded his mount and the horses waded across the stream. They rode out of the wooded area, crossed some more rangeland and topped a rise. In a meadow below them Kathy saw a herd of cattle grazing. But not ordinary cattle. These looked like something out of an old-time photograph.

"They're longhorns!" Kathy exclaimed, hardly able to believe her eyes.

"They sure are. Look at that fellow down there. I bet his horns span fifteen feet."

"That's a rare sight."

"Oh, there are still a few longhorns around. It started out as a nostalgic hobby but some ranchers have the notion that it might be a practical idea and are rebuilding herds of them. For a long time, heavy beef cattle were so popular and the longhorns were dying out. Now, with people worrying about cholesterol, some cattlemen are getting interested in a leaner breed. Longhorns fit the bill."

"Where on earth did you get them?"

"Heard about them at a cattle auction. I probably paid too much for them, but what the heck."

Kathy smiled. "My grandfather told me a lot of stories about longhorns, what incredible survivors they were."

"They were survivors all right. They could live in the thorny thickets of the brush country, fight off predators with those long horns and make it through drought cycles by climbing mesquite trees to get the beans and eating prickly pears, thorns and all."

"I'd like to see my fat, lazy Santa Gertrudis do that!"

"Do you have very many?"

"Just a small herd."

They rode slowly back to Dak's house, talking about cattle and ranching, carefully keeping the conversation on safe, impersonal subjects. Kathy found herself relating in the old companionship she and Dak had once shared.

As they approached the ranch yard, Dak turned his face toward her. "I wish you'd reconsider having supper with us. It would mean a lot to Joedy. And it would give me a chance to repay you for being so nice to the boy."

Dak was looking straight at her, his gaze catching her eyes in a disconcerting manner. When he looked at her like that she was unable to think clearly. "All right," she said before she could get her thoughts organized, then instantly regretted it. But it was too late to back out. "I'll—I'll have to take my horse back to my place and get cleaned up. Will seven o'clock be all right?"

"Perfect." Dak smiled. "Joedy will be in seventh heaven."

Dak watched Kathy ride away. The sight of her trim figure astride her horse, riding with graceful ease, filled him with a mixture of strong, conflicting emotions.

Since he'd returned to Endless, he'd thought a lot about those times ten years ago, about the hard, grueling hours he had put in training for the Olympics, about how important that win had been to him. Winning the gold medal had meant the difference between a life of success or failure.

Seeing the tired, defeated look on his father's face had spurred him on, fueling his anger at Burke Ayers, pumping adrenaline through his body when he had needed the extra spurt of energy.

He'd won at the Olympics, but Burke Ayers had won out in the end. Dak knew, when he was turned down for job after job, that Burke Ayers had put the word out not to hire him.

Burke hadn't been able to squelch his triumphant return to Endless, but that night the town gave a dance in Dak's honor. He'd wanted Kathy at his side more than anything. Until then, he'd kept a rein on his emotions with Kathy. It hadn't been easy, loving her and wanting her the way he had, but he loved her too much to tie her down to a guy who was a failure. He'd seen the hope go out of his mother's eyes as year after year their little farm went downhill. He was either going to give Kathy the best or nothing. And after his big win, he felt worthy of her. In the flush of victory, he planned to propose.

But she turned down his request for a date. Instead, she showed up at the dance with Brice Williams. Dak had been jealous and furious. Unreasonably so, he admitted now. He wouldn't even listen to her explanation about how her father had given her the alternative of going to the dance with Brice or staying home. It only made him madder that she was so wishy-washy when it came to standing up to Burke Ayers.

The next morning, Dak flew to California without saying goodbye. By the time he stepped off the plane, he was regretting his rash actions. He was missing Kathy already. He tried calling her and when he couldn't get her on the phone, he wrote a long letter of apology. He told her how much he loved her and that he wanted to marry her. He told her that as soon as he got settled and was earning some money, he was going to send her a plane ticket and hoped she would join him. That was only the first of a string of letters he sent her, all saying the same thing. But she never answered.

He tried phoning. Each time he was told she wasn't home. He left word for her to return his calls. She never did.

Months went by. Then he ran into a friend from Endless who told him that Kathy was engaged to Brice Williams, ending Dak's hopes that they could patch things up. Soon after, he had married Linda Davis, an aspiring young actress.

Now Kathy was telling him she had never gotten the letters. It was quite possible her father had intercepted the letters and the phone calls. The tough old rancher had been dead set against Dak as a suitor for his daughter's hand. Dak was sure he was delighted when his daughter's boyfriend had left town.

Dak experienced an almost unbearable wave of sadness and regret when he thought about the lost years, about how things might have been if Kathy had answered his letters, if she had joined him in California. They would have been married. Joedy might have been their son.

Remorse filled his heart as he thought about his marriage to Linda. At the time, he had blamed their problems on Linda's life-style and the Hollywood crowd she hung out with. She was a beautiful, ambitious girl with a fair degree of acting talent.

Dak had been an outsider, a small-town boy who had been thrust into the national limelight. His healthy good looks and fame had attracted Linda who loved being with the beautiful people. But after the first excitement of marriage faded, she had grown cool. From worlds apart, they were totally mismatched. Linda would have left him then, but she discovered she was pregnant with Joedy. She hadn't wanted to get pregnant; Joedy had been an accident. She'd resented the pregnancy, but when Joedy was born, she loved him. In her own way she was a good mother. As her movie and TV career gained momentum, she was gone much of the time, but when she was home, she showered Joedy with love and attention. Dak would always give her credit for that.

Thinking about Joedy now, Dak unsaddled his horse and went into the house. He walked upstairs and peered through the partly opened door into Joedy's room. The boy was seated in front of a desk cluttered with books and partly finished model airplanes. In the center of all the clutter was a framed picture of his mother. Joedy sat quietly, arms folded on the desk, chin resting on his arms, staring at the picture. Dak sighed. He had seen Joedy sit like this, staring at the picture by the hour.

Hearing him, Joedy turned. His eyes were red from crying. The sight made Dak's heart wrench. He drew a breath, hoping the news he was bringing would make the boy feel better. "Guess what, Joedy. We're going to have company for supper."

The boy's eyes brightened at once. "Miss Ayers?"

"Yep. She went home to change, but she'll be back about seven. Now scoot into the bathroom and get cleaned up. You'll want to look nice for our guest."

When Kathy returned to her ranch, she unsaddled her horse, gave him some feed, then went into her house to shower and change. After a refreshing shower, she brushed her hair until the mane of dark strands shone with highlights, applied makeup lightly, then put on a summery dress with spaghetti straps that left her shoulders bare. Glancing in a full-length mirror, she blushed at the utterly feminine reflection, remembering all too well the fluttery sensation she had once felt inside when she dressed for a date with Dak. Angry with herself, she grabbed her car keys and left the house.

Chapter Six

After Joedy started taking his shower, Dak went downstairs to let the cook know they were having a guest for supper.

They agreed on steak, salad, baked potatoes and asparagus and José promised one of his pastry specialties for dessert. Then Dak went upstairs to take his shower. He experienced a pleasant feeling of anticipation at the prospect of having Kathy over for dinner. It had been a long time since he had enjoyed the company of a woman, not since Linda's death. For the last year, he had been too wrapped up with Joedy's emotional problems and the details of buying this ranch and moving to think about the opposite sex.

Dak dressed in sharply creased tan slacks and a casual, short-sleeved white sport shirt. He stood at the window and watched Kathy drive into the yard promptly at seven, just as a sudden summer shower began falling. Dak grabbed an umbrella and ran out to her car.

"Where did this come from?" she exclaimed as she ducked out of her car and under the umbrella with Dak. "There wasn't a cloud in the sky when I left home."

They hurried up to the porch. Dak closed the umbrella, shaking it out and dropping it in a stand by the door. He turned and, for a moment, the sight of Kathy took his breath away. She was wearing a wisp of a dress that left her shoulders bare. Raindrops sparkled in her hair like diamonds. Her cheeks were flushed and her breathing was slightly accelerated from the dash to the porch. The swift rise and fall of her breasts strained the confines of the thin dress. The fragrance of her perfume surrounded her with an aura of femininity. She was utterly lovely, Dak thought, drawn to her.

She glanced up, her eyes looking straight into his. The color of her cheeks grew more flushed. Then she looked quickly away. "Where's Joedy?" she asked. He thought her voice sounded slightly unsteady.

"Making sure he's fit to come downstairs to dinner." Dak grinned. "You won't recognize him with the dust and dirt washed off."

They walked into the house as Joedy was coming down the stairs, three at a time. "Hi," he said breathlessly.

"Well, hi, yourself," Kathy exclaimed. "My, don't you look nice!"

Joedy looked scrubbed and neat with his cowlick brushed down and temporarily in place.

"Tell you what," Dak said. "I need to let my cook know you're here. Joedy, why don't you show Miss Kathy your new computer while I have a word with José."

"All right." Joedy led the way up the stairs and pushed open his bedroom door.

It was a typical boy's room, cluttered with toys, books and clothes. Several posters of movie and rock music stars adorned the walls.

"Here's my new computer," Joedy said, leading the way to a desk. "My dad bought it for me last month. I have a bunch of games. Maybe you could play some with me sometime?"

"That might be fun." Kathy judged the computer to be quite elaborate as were the toys she saw in the room. Dak was obviously sparing no expense in an attempt to overcome Joedy's depression.

Then she saw a framed photograph of a lovely young woman on the boy's desk.

"That's my mom," Joedy said. A shadow passed over his face. His eyes lost their luster.

An odd sadness gripped Kathy as she looked at the picture of Dak's wife. She had been a remarkably beautiful woman. What had their marriage been like, she wondered. Had Dak loved her deeply? Was he grieving for her the way Joedy was?

Uncomfortable, Kathy felt like an intruder. She gave Joedy a concerned look, wondering what she should say. She had the feeling that Joedy had withdrawn inside himself.

"Hey, I believe the rain is letting up," she said a little too brightly, going to the window. "Come have a look."

Joedy followed her, but he was quiet now. It wasn't until they were seated at the supper table that he began talking again.

Kathy found it difficult to relax. She was very conscious of Dak's disturbing presence. She found that the safest course was to remain impersonal.

"How are your parents, Dak?"

"They're well. They're living in California now."

"Yes, I remember when they moved away from here several years ago."

Dak nodded. "I was in a position to buy them a little place in the valley. They have a few acres where Dad can tinker with a garden. He's like a boy with a new scooter. My mother has the kind of home she always wanted. She looks ten years younger."

"I'm glad," Kathy said with all her heart. She had known Dak's parents all her life and they'd treated her like a daughter. She'd always thought the couple shared a special kind of love. She could remember the tender look that filled Dak's father's eyes when he looked at his wife; he was obviously as much in love with her as he'd been on the day they were married.

"Y'know, I had a special feeling for your parents," Kathy said. She almost added that she'd envied Dak having a mother because she'd had to grow up without one, but she caught herself, remembering Joedy. That gave her a sudden insight. Perhaps that was why she'd formed such an immediate attachment for the boy. She'd been about his age, perhaps a year or two younger, when she'd lost her mother. She knew from firsthand experience what he was going through. She looked at him with a fresh understanding. "What do you think of your grandparents, Joedy?"

"They're keen. I'm going out to visit them in about a month. Grandad is going to take me for a ride on his new tractor."

Kathy smiled, some of her anger at Dak softening. He might have left her high and dry, but he'd been a good son to his parents. "I'm glad things have worked out for them. I know they were having a tough struggle when they lived here."

"Yes, they were," Dak said, a sudden bitterness in his voice. "I'm grateful that I was able to make things a little better for them."

Kathy was startled by the intensity of Dak's response, then she remembered the cloud of poverty that had hung over the Roberts's home when he was growing up. She suspected it had given him the obsessive drive to overcome any obstacles that stood in his way.

She changed the subject. "I understand you own a chain of health studios on the West Coast."

"I did. I sold out before I moved back here." Then Dak gazed at her with a look of amused interest. "And you have become a lady barrister, and a very good one, I understand."

"Does that surprise you?"

"In a way, I guess it does. I keep trying to fit the image of a lady Perry Mason onto the memory I have of a bubbleheaded teenager."

"What d'you mean, bubbleheaded? I was vale-dictorian, if you'll remember."

"Yes, so you were. Your grandfather on your mother's side was a lawyer, wasn't he?"

Kathy nodded. "He was special to me and I was his favorite grandchild. I'm sure he had a lot to do with my deciding to go into law. My grandfather and great-grandfather on Dad's side were all ranchers."

"Yeah, cattle barons, the big *patrons*. They owned the land and the people around here," Dak growled menacingly.

Kathy gave him a dark look. A hot retort was on the tip of her tongue, but she didn't want to upset Joedy by starting a row with Dak. Despite her hair-trigger temper, she somehow managed to swallow her angry words and pointedly ignored Dak for the rest of the meal, giving Joedy her full attention.

After supper, she played some computer games with Joedy and read him a story until Dak came up to his room and told Joedy it was bedtime.

"Aw, Dad!"

"You've had a long day, son."

"Your dad is right, Joedy," Kathy agreed. "That long ride over to my place, and then having to run away from the Indians."

Joedy's gaze lowered. "There weren't really any Indians," he mumbled.

"There weren't?" Kathy asked, sounding surprised.

"Naw. I—I guess I was kind of pretending."

"Well, pretending is a lot of fun. I do it all the time. Just so we know what's make-believe and what's for real, huh?"

Joedy nodded. "Yeah."

Dak was looking at the boy with a strange expression. Kathy thought she saw the glint of tears in his eyes.

"Well, you let your dad tuck you in for the night," she said.

"Will you come see me again soon?"

"Sure. Maybe you can come over to my place for a visit again. But this time, tell your dad where you're going, okay?"

"Okay."

Kathy gave him a good-night kiss. For a moment his arms went shyly around her neck.

Leaving Dak alone with Joedy, she went downstairs and stepped out on the porch. The summer shower had ended and the sky was now clear and sparkling with stars. Water dripped softly from wet leaves. The air smelled clean and the fragrance of Texas wildflowers wafted across the prairie.

It was a beautiful night. Kathy stepped down from the porch and walked across the yard to the corral.

For reasons totally beyond her ability to comprehend, she felt close to tears.

For a long time, she leaned against a corner of the corral, gazing up at the stars, lost in thought. The sound of a footstep crunching a twig startled her out of her reverie and she spun around.

Dak's broad shoulders were outlined against the stars. "You startled me," she said.

"Sorry. I thought you heard me coming."

"I guess I was off in another world. Have any trouble getting Joedy to sleep?"

"Are you kidding? That boy was worn out. He was asleep the minute he hit the bed."

She became aware of Dak's steady gaze. His intense scrutiny made her painfully self-conscious and she looked away. Then she heard Dak's voice, thick with emotion. "Kathy, I can't tell you how grateful I am over what you've done for Joedy."

"I haven't done anything except be friends with him and that's certainly not hard to do."

"I don't guess you realize what a change has come over him. I can't tell you how I felt tonight when he admitted he made up the story about the Indians. It's the most encouraging sign I've seen that he's getting better. You've got some kind of magic where he's concerned."

"We understand each other. I—I had a bit of insight tonight. It could have something to do with the fact that I lost my mother when I was about his age. I guess I know how he feels and he senses that."

"Well, it looks right now as if you're taking the place of his mother. I hope that's okay with you."

"I—I guess so," Kathy said with a sudden feeling of uneasiness. "You're laying quite a responsibility on me."

"Not at all. You don't have to do anything, except be yourself with Joedy. Maybe you could see your way clear to spend a little time with him now and then? It would mean a lot."

"Yes, certainly."

"The FHA is going to sponsor a children's rodeo later this summer. I'd like to enter Joedy in the competition. I think it would be good for him to compete. Junior Gomez, one of my hands, has offered to give Joedy roping lessons. If you could spare the time to drop over and watch Joedy practice, I think it would encourage him to try harder."

"All right. Sure."

After that, the subject of Joedy seemed to have been exhausted and Kathy stiffened. She fumbled for a subject to steer them away from themselves. "The supper was delicious, by the way. Those pastries were out of this world. Where on earth did you acquire a cook like that?"

"I'm not real sure," Dak said with a chuckle. "He came with the place. One of my other hands said he'd been a chef at a big restaurant in Mexico City."

"I can believe it. He looks like an outlaw, but boy can he cook!"

"I know. At first I was afraid to fire him. Now I don't want to. Actually, I don't think he's as fierce as he looks. He has the soul of an artist. You should see the delicate figures of horses he carves out of wood. He carved one for Joedy that ought to go in an art gallery."

"You just never can judge people by appearances, can you?"

Dak leaned on the fence beside her. She was aware of his broad shoulder touching hers. The male scent of his body was in her nostrils. She could feel the warmth of him, so close. All of her senses tingled. The beauty of the rain-washed evening, the darkness, the intimacy of their solitude were starting to create a powerful mood.

"Lovely evening," Dak said softly. "I like it after a shower. The whole world seems clean and fresh. Remember how we liked to play in the rain?"

"I remember when you pushed me into a mud puddle and your mother spanked you."

Dak laughed. "As I recall, I had good provocation. My mother didn't know that a few minutes before you had dumped a bucket of rainwater over my head."

Kathy grinned. "I'm sure I had a reason for doing it."

"Well, it was quite a few years ago. I seem to remember you got me in quite a bit of trouble when we were growing up."

"Like what?"

"Well, it was usually that temper of yours. Like the time you hit me over the head with your geography book and the teacher made us stay after school to clean blackboard erasers."

"I hit you with my geography book because you wrote 'Kathy Ayers loves Vernon Stutler' on the side of the gym."

"I do seem to remember something about that," Dak admitted. "Poor Vernon. He was the brunt of everybody's joke because he was fat and dumb. No wonder you hit me with your geography book."

"He's not so fat and dumb now. I saw him at the class reunion the other night. He's running a very successful automobile dealership in San Antonio."

"So I heard. Maybe you should have stuck with Vernon."

Kathy gave him a playful shove. "Lucky for you I don't have a geography book handy."

"I was glad to see that most of our school crowd has done all right for themselves since graduation, like good old Vernon Stutler. By the way, I hear you were the chairman of the reunion committee. You did a nice job. The decorations in the gym were great. Everything went smoothly."

"Thank you."

"Seeing our classmates at the reunion brought back a lot of memories."

"I know what you mean. The pep rallies, the football games . . . proms."

"Cramming for exams," Dak added.

"And the gossip about who was dating whom, and what couple was going steady."

"I can hear the lockers slamming in the halls now," Dak said. A low chuckle sounded from his throat.

"Good old Endless High. We thought those times would last forever," Kathy said a bit sadly.

"Remember our school pep song?"

"Are you kidding? Of course I remember." Softly, she began singing, "On the field our boys will fight . . .

"Glory in the gold and white. . . ."

The sentimental mood had broken down the wall between them. He had been a playmate when they were growing up. Then suddenly they were in high school and one day her feelings for Dak changed and she was shy and self-conscious around him. She thought about him constantly.

Dak's intense gaze brought it all back now as they sang the school song together.

The song ended. There was a lengthy silence and she seemed to hear the seconds ticking by. His eyes took in the outline of her face, then trailed down her throat to the swell of her breast, her waist, the curving lines of her thighs outlined by her thin dress. Her heart beat rapidly, pumping warm blood through her veins, flushing her cheeks.

"Remember the time we went skinny-dipping in the Nueces River?" Dak teased softly.

Her cheeks got hot and she closed her eyes in confusion. "We were kids—six or seven years old...."

"So we were. Innocent kids, just starting to find out about life. Too bad people can't stay kids forever."

Did she hear a note of regret in his voice?

He touched her arm, his sure fingers sending a vibrating tingle through her body. Her breathing became difficult. The evening was taking a course she hadn't anticipated. She wanted to draw back, turn away from him, but found herself captive to the starry night . . . to Dak.

Dak's fingers trailed down her arm to her hand resting on the corral fence. She couldn't make her hand move. His fingers laced through hers, gave them a squeeze, and gently he pulled her around to face him and slipped his other arm lightly around her waist.

"Dak . . ." she protested weakly.

His gaze, stormy now, intensified. Tenderly, he touched her hair. "You're as lovely as you were on graduation night, Kathy."

"Don't let the moonlight fool you," she said unsteadily. "I'm no longer a high school girl. I'm starting to get a few lines around my eyes. . . ."

He didn't seem to be listening. He drew her closer until her body touched his, her breasts against his broad chest, her thighs against his, burning through the fabric.

She looked wide-eyed into the depths of his tortured gaze. Then with a muffled cry, his lips touched hers. They had not kissed in ten years. Her mouth remembered the feel of his, welcomed it hungrily. His embrace tightened and she was pressed against him.

It was different now. Their high school kisses had been sweet and exciting with a promise of unknown thrills. Her body had just begun to awaken to passion. But now she was a woman, with a woman's response to desire. Dak's kiss aroused her fiercely. Her breasts swelled and ached. Her nerves tingled; her body throbbed with desire. She welcomed the pressure of his thighs against hers.

Dak's lips moved over her cheeks. Her head fell back, offering her throat and his kisses found the soft hollow there. Her blood thundered in her ears as his fingers pushed the thin straps of her dress from her shoulder. The top of her dress fell down. She shuddered as his kisses sent a fiery trail from her shoulder down the hollow between her breasts.

With a gasp, she came to her senses. She drew away from him, pulling up her dress as she stumbled blindly across the yard. Her name echoed harshly in the night and she heard him hurrying after her, but she didn't look back. Half-blinded with tears, she threw herself in her car, backed out of the yard and started home.

She was shaking from head to foot. Dak still had the power to drive her out of her mind with hunger for him. He had broken her heart once. With a terrified heart, she prayed she was not going to let him do it again.

Dak watched the taillights of Kathy's car disappear down the road. Then he sat down on the ranch-house-porch steps and leaned against a post. He had been profoundly moved by their kiss, their closeness tonight. He could still feel the warmth of Kathy's lips, the soft contours of her body pressed against his, the seductive fragrance of her perfume. The kiss had left him shaken and hungry for more....

There was no avoiding the truth about himself and Kathy. The feeling was still there, the passion stronger than ever. Ten years apart had meant nothing. The way Kathy had responded—the eager hunger in her lips, the trembling need of her body—he was certain she must feel the same.

He closed his eyes, reliving the thrill of the moment, tormenting himself with fantasies of what would have happened if Kathy hadn't broken away.

Why had she fled? That wasn't hard to understand. She probably hadn't been prepared for the intensity of the passion that flared between them any more than he had. He suspected that she had needed to put a safe distance between them so she could think rationally and figure out where tonight was taking them.

He needed to so the same, but at the moment he was content just to let the dust settle.

Chapter Seven

He what?" Kathy exploded.

"I just came from the courthouse. Dak Roberts has filed for the mayor's race," Arthur Peters repeated, dropping down into a chair in her office.

Kathy stared at her campaign manager with a dazed expression. Slowly, disbelievingly, she shook her head. "I can't grasp it. Why in heaven's name is Dak Roberts getting into the mayoral race? What has gotten into him?"

"I don't know."

"I've talked with him several times this week. He didn't say a thing about it. We didn't even talk about the city election."

Peters looked as baffled as she. "Maybe it was a last-minute decision. He got in just under the filing deadline."

As the first shock of numbed disbelief subsided, Kathy burned with betrayal and anger. "Either it was a last-minute, spur-of-the-moment decision as you say, or the rat knew good and well all week what he was going to do and didn't bother mentioning it to me!" she exploded.

"Well, whatever his reason, we now have problems," her campaign manager said.

Arthur Peters was a small, nervous man who shifted uncomfortably as he talked. He was semi-retired from a thriving farm-implement business that he had started twenty years ago. Now that his son was able to take over the business, Arthur could devote more of his time to his real love, politics. For years he had been active in local political circles, having worked as a precinct chairman, poll watcher and local party chairman, and had been the campaign manager for several state legislators.

He went on, "I felt confident you'd have a good chance against Henry Jimpson. People are getting a bit tired of Henry after ten years. He's a terrible old stick-in-the-mud. The main problem, of course, was getting the voters around here to accept the idea of a woman mayor. That's quite a big step for a conservative community like Endless."

"I know," Kathy said grimly. "We hadn't had a woman on the city council until we got Sarah Tussey. When she won a seat in the last election it shook up some of the old mossbacks around here."

"Exactly. So, that was the thing we had to run against more than running against old Henry—getting the folks here to swallow the idea of a woman being mayor. I think we could have pulled it off, though, if nobody else entered the race."

"And now somebody has."

"Dak Roberts," Arthur continued, slowly shaking his head.

Kathy threw a pencil down on her desk. "What does Dak Roberts know about being mayor of Endless?" she cried bitterly.

"Beats me." Arthur shrugged.

"Surely the voters will realize that. I'm much more qualified—"

"Trouble is," Peters interrupted glumly, "Dak's awfully well-liked around here. Y'know—local boy makes good. He's something of a local celebrity. That can add up to a lot of votes."

Kathy's lips were pressed together in an angry line. She shook her head and turned to the picture window behind her desk, looking down at the town that had been her home all her life. "Endless deserves more than a glamour boy," she growled, her temper reaching the boiling point. "We're going to be facing a lot of problems in the next few years—we need a new water treatment plant. Streets need repairing. Those things cost money. It means a bond issue and the raising of property taxes, but they're issues that have to be faced. Our city council has been too chicken to face the facts. The council needs someone to light a fire under them."

"I know, I know." Peters sighed. "Running on campaign promises to raise taxes isn't the best way to get votes, though. Not if you're up against someone as popular as Dak Roberts."

"I wonder who's backing him? I thought we had most of the established business community solidly behind me."

"I'm trying to find out. Could be the younger professionals and business people in the area."

"I'm going to have a talk with Dak," Kathy exclaimed. She told her secretary to cancel appointments for the rest of the afternoon, grabbed her purse and stormed out of the office.

On her drive out to Dak's ranch, tears stung Kathy's eyes as she thought back to that fatal kiss. She had driven home in an emotional tailspin that ranged from ecstatic happiness to a whole new set of uncertainties. Sleep had eluded her all night.

Dak phoned her early the next morning. His voice was warm and tender, like a caress. "Hi, Kathy Ayers. How are you this morning?"

"As well as can be expected. I hardly slept."

"I know what you mean. I sat out on the porch until nearly dawn, thinking about us. Kathy, I want to see you today."

"Oh, no," she said with instant fright. "You keep your distance, Dak Roberts, until I have a chance to get my life back in order. If you come over here I won't have a rational thought in my head."

Dak laughed softly. "Well, that's encouraging. But what do you have to think about?"

"Plenty! You've come back after ten years and turned my world upside down."

There was a moment's silence. "Is that good or bad?"

"Good and bad, I guess. I don't mind telling you I'm a little shook up. Yesterday morning, my life was on a nice, even, predictable course. Now I don't know where I'm going."

"I can tell you where you're going. You don't think you can walk away from that kiss last night, do you?"

"No," she admitted shakily.

"Then, where you're going is right back into my arms to take up where we left off. Why did you run away like that, anyway?"

Kathy's cheeks flamed. Her intense desire for him brought a mixture of pain and fear. "You know good and well why," she said thickly. "A few more minutes with you and we would have passed the point of no return."

Dak chuckled. "That would have been so bad?"

Hot blood coursed through her veins. She pushed the sheet off. "No," she murmured. "It wouldn't have been so bad. In fact, I suspect it would have been pretty good. But I'm not going to run back into your arms, Dak. Not after all that has happened. I'm not going to wake up again to find out you've pulled another disappearing act."

"Are you going to hold that against me forever?"

"I'm not holding a grudge. But, Dak, I'm not a high school girl with a blind crush anymore. I'm a grown woman and I need to know where all this is taking us. I haven't seen you in ten years. You're something of a stranger to me now. I keep thinking about us the way we were ten years ago. All that reminiscing got to me, but a lot of water has gone under the dam since high school, things that could have changed you a lot. I'm not in the sixth grade, hitting you with my geography book, and you're not my date to the senior prom. I need time to find out what kind of a person you are now."

There was a short silence. "I understand, Kathy," Dak said gently. "I really don't think we're all that different from back then. But maybe I am rushing things a bit. I guess I have to give you time to get used to the idea of us back together again. I'll be a good boy and play it cool, but when am I going to see you again?"

Kathy smiled fondly. "Pretty soon. Why don't we keep it to telephone calls for a couple of days? Then we'll see."

"Okay. Tell you what—maybe you could come over one afternoon this week and watch Joedy practice his roping. It would mean a lot to him. And it would mean a lot for me to see you...."

"How can I turn down an offer like that?" she said lightly.

On Tuesday afternoon, she had driven over to Dak's ranch. She and Dak sat on the top rail of the corral fence, holding hands as they watched Junior Gomez give Joedy his first lessons in handling a lariat. That was when Dak pressed Kathy for another date and she'd agreed to have dinner with him Friday.

And now she was on the way to his ranch again, but in an entirely different frame of mind. She clasped the steering wheel as if she wished it were Dak's neck she was wringing.

She drove into the yard in a cloud of dust and slammed the car door behind her as she jumped out and headed toward the house. There she was told by one of the ranch hands that Dak was in the barn so she rounded the house in angry strides. Dak was inside, stripped to the waist, forking some hay into a stall. Gleaming with perspiration, his powerful muscles rippled smoothly. For just a second, the sight of all that raw masculinity took her breath away. Then she remembered why she was there and she got mad all over again.

"Dak Roberts," she began resolutely, "I want to have a word with you."

He put down his pitchfork, drawing the back of his hand across his sweaty forehead. He smiled, not taking his eyes off her as he reached for his shirt. "This is a surprise. I'm glad to see you, Kathy, but if you'd let me know you were coming, I could have made myself a little more presentable. I thought our date was for tomorrow night."

"It *was* for tomorrow night."

He drew his shirt on lazily, looking at her with a quizzical expression. "What do you mean?"

"I mean you have some tall explaining to do or you can forget about us."

"Explaining?"

"I've been informed this afternoon that you intend to enter the mayor's race."

He nodded slowly. "That's right."

Her dark eyes blazed. "A little item you seemed to have overlooked mentioning to me."

"Well, I guess I should have talked it over with you, but it was kind of a last-minute decision. I have been giving it considerable thought. Some people have approached me and urged me to run. Today was the deadline for filing, and I made the decision just this morning to go ahead."

She stared at him, shaking her head in disbelief. "I hoped there might be some kind of mistake. Dak, what kind of grandstand play is this?"

Some of the humor faded from his eyes and he began to get angry. "I don't think I care for your choice of words, Kathy. There isn't any grandstanding. I had to be committed or I wouldn't have taken this step."

"Dak, you know absolutely nothing about being mayor of this town. It takes a few qualifications besides jumping off a diving board."

His face flushed angrily. "Suppose we let the voters decide if I'm qualified or not."

In her agitation, Kathy paced back and forth. "You might very well win this election. That's what makes me so mad! You're something of a hero around here. You could quite easily win an election on the basis of your popularity."

Dak gave her a searching look. "Sounds like we're getting to what's really got you mad. You thought you had the election sewed up, and now you think you might lose. Sounds like sour grapes to me, Kathy."

"No, what's really got me mad is that you're butting into local politics, which you know nothing about, for some frivolous reason that makes no sense whatever."

"I have a very good reason. I'll tell you exactly why I want to run and why other people want me to run. I think it's high time somebody who doesn't have the last name of Ayers had something to say about things around town. Your father has been the *patron* of this community for thirty years. Every city official from the dogcatcher on up had the Ayers stamp of approval. Henry Jimpson never opened his mouth on any issue without consulting your father first. If you get elected, Burke Ayers'll be behind you, too."

"He will not! Get that stupid notion out of your head, Dak Roberts. I've grown up. I do things my way now."

"I'm not convinced. I don't think anyone else could win, not with your father behind you. I might be the only one who could pull it off."

"What is this thing you have against my father, anyway?"

"He broke us up didn't he?"

"What do you mean? You have some kind of vendetta against my family that I don't understand."

"I'm not alone. I told you a number of people have come to me, promising support if I'd run for the office."

"Well, this shows me that you don't really care about us!" she said bitterly.

"You're wrong, Kathy. I care about our relationship a great deal. That's one important reason I'm doing this. I can foresee a lot of trouble for us if you get into a political situation where you're still under your father's thumb. Maybe you've grown up, but I'm not convinced. I think deep down, you're still Daddy's little girl."

"He doesn't run me, Dak Roberts!"

Dak's eyes searched her face. "I'm not so sure of that. He was always ambitious for you. That was one reason he tried to break us up."

"One reason? You're implying there was another?"

If Dak heard the probing question in her reply, he ignored it. "It was your father's idea for you to go on to college and get your law degree, wasn't it?"

Kathy's eyes glared back at his, meeting his challenge. "I don't see anything wrong with a father having ambitions for his daughter. Yes, he did have hopes I'd get a law degree. But if you think I did it just to please him, you're dead wrong. I decided on my own that was what I wanted or I never would have done it."

Dak looked as if he didn't believe her. "How about this idea of your running for mayor?" he asked. "I suspect it was your father who put that idea in your head."

"Certainly not!"

"Are you sure, Kathy? Think about it for a minute. We're not always aware of how other people can influence our lives. Are you dead certain he didn't drop a little remark here and there that it was time Endless had a new mayor?"

"He might have said something like that," Kathy admitted. "I can't remember everything we talked about. But that doesn't prove anything—"

"How about his hinting that you ought to consider running for the office?"

"You sound like a prosecutor putting somebody on the witness stand!" Kathy fumed.

"You aren't answering my question."

"I don't have to stand here and be cross-examined by you, Dak Roberts," Kathy snapped, her eyes bright with angry tears. "Your insinuations are insulting. It's obvious now that I was foolish to think we could rekindle an old high school romance. Perhaps I never really was in love with you."

She turned to leave, but Dak caught her arm. She tried to wrench away, but he held her firmly.

"Cool down that temper, Kathy. You don't mean what you said. You couldn't have kissed me the way you did the other night if you didn't want me as much as I want you."

"You caught me in a weak moment!" she retorted, her eyes flashing. "The moonlight, the wild flowers, all that sentimental talk about old friends, old memories.... My brain must have turned to mush. But it won't happen again—you can bet on that!"

"I wouldn't give odds on that kind of a bet," Dak murmured. For a long, painful moment, his eyes looked deep into hers. The space between them vibrated with emotional tension.

Dak smiled, his voice soft now. "Why don't we make it a friendly race?"

With that, he suddenly swept Kathy up in his arms, giving her a kiss that left her breathless. She was too surprised at first to resist. When she got her wits about her, she tried to struggle, but the effort was useless against Dak's powerful arms. He kissed her again.

She was furious with her body that grew weak and trembled in his embrace, melting against him, molding her pliant curves against his hard muscles. She fought against her own responses that wanted her lips to soften and part under his. She fought—and lost.

The kiss became more heated. Once again, she felt the heat of desire overwhelming her defenses. They sank down on a bed of hay. Dimly she realized Dak had unbuttoned first his shirt and then her blouse, pushing it down from her shoulders. Her quivering breasts brushed against his chest. She clung to him as the kiss deepened, her lips parting under his, welcoming the thrust of his tongue. Her lungs strained for breath and her heart pounded, pumping blood through her in heated waves.

Dak held her in the passionate embrace for endless moments as her desire grew until it became unbearable.

Finally, he released her. For a moment she lay in his arms, too weak to move. Then she rose to her feet, her legs barely able to support her. Her lips were red and swollen from his kisses and she avoided his eyes as her trembling fingers fastened the buttons on her blouse.

Dak reclined on the hay, gazing at her with an amused expression. She looked away, anger and humiliation flushing her cheeks.

"After that kiss, don't you think we ought to patch things up?" he suggested.

She gave him a scathing look. "Maybe we could...if you'd withdraw from the race."

"I was going to suggest you withdraw," he countered. "That would prove to me you really are out from under your father's foot."

"I am not withdrawing from the race!" she choked. "I'm going to run and I'm going to beat you, Dak Roberts!"

"Well," he sighed, sitting up, "may the best man—or woman—win."

Chapter Eight

A week had passed since Dak entered the mayor's race. It had been a busy week for him, setting up campaign headquarters in a vacant storefront in town, meeting with various civic leaders and people supporting his candidacy, organizing campaign workers. His business experience was useful to him now. He had learned a lot about delegating responsibilities, spotting the movers and shakers.

By the end of the week he had a publicity chairman, a campaign manager and a fund-raising chairman lined up. His campaign was under way and rolling.

Dak's manager was Cliff Dunlap, the high school principal who had spearheaded the effort to get Dak to run in the first place. He had made numerous trips out to Dak's ranch, bringing with him various community leaders. Now that Dak had officially filed, Cliff demonstrated his commitment by giving up his summer vacation to devote all his time and energy to the campaign.

Today at a noon luncheon of the Endless Civitan Club, Dak was scheduled to make his first speech. Cliff had coached him the night before.

"This one is important, Dak," he said. "Most of the businessmen and professionals in town will be there. The majority of them, of course, have done business with the Ayers family for years. But they also know and like you."

Cliff Dunlap had gotten his master's degree from Baylor University. He'd worked on his doctorate in the summers while teaching at a small school in West Texas. Two years ago, he'd been hired to fill the job of principal of Endless High. At thirty, he was the youngest principal the school had ever had. He'd faced the difficult job of adapting school policy to the tough guidelines of the new Texas school-reform laws, especially in conforming to the "no pass, no play" ruling that removed students from extra curricular activities if they received a failing grade. In a

town the size of Endless, where the outcome of the
Friday night high school football game could affect
the mood of the entire community, it had not been
easy to bench the star fullback. Somehow Cliff had
managed to do it and still remain popular; his per-
suasive personality had won out. Now his energy was
directed toward Dak.

At first, Dak had resisted the idea of running for
mayor wholeheartedly. "I just want to run my ranch
and take care of my son."

"Dak, if you're going to be a part of this community, you owe it your full commitment. This town
has been under the thumb of the Ayers family too
long. It needs a change."

"I'll certainly agree with you there," Dak had admitted. "But Cliff, you've come to the wrong guy.
First of all, I don't want to run against Kathy Ayers
for personal reasons. Besides, she's much more
qualified for the job—she's a successful attorney.
Kathy has lived here all her life. I grew up here, but
I've been away for ten years. That makes me something of a newcomer."

"Not really. Everybody in town knows and ad-
mires you, Dak. With all the political influence
Burke Ayers has around here, I doubt if anyone else
in town would have a chance against Kathy. But I

think you might be able to pull it off. That's why we're so very anxious to get you to run.''

''Who's 'we'? Who else besides you would vote for me?''

''Quite a few people—especially the younger voters, men and women your age, Dak, who went to school with you here, or, like myself, who have moved here in the last few years. Our generation hasn't bowed to the patronage of the big ranchers.''

''Doesn't sound as if you have much use for Kathy's father,'' Dak observed.

''Oh, I don't have a thing against the man personally. Matter of fact, there are a lot of things I have to admire about him. He's certainly not stingy with his money. The Ayers family has been most generous with this community. The Ayers foundation built our hospital. It's just that many of the younger people like myself want to have a say in how the town is run.''

''Kathy Ayers is young. She's my age.''

''But she's an Ayers. Don't you think if she's elected, her father will still be the power behind the throne, so to speak?''

Dak frowned. ''He certainly will.''

''A lot of people see her father behind her.''

''Yes, and that bothers me,'' Dak agreed. ''I'll have to tell you, frankly, Cliff, that I've had my own dealings with Burke Ayers. So has my family." Dak's jaw tightened as he thought about his father and the hard times that had been forced on him. "You're right when you say Burke Ayers can be generous," Dak went on quietly, "and he can also be vindictive. I have my own personal score to settle with Burke Ayers. No one around here would like more than I to see him taken down a few notches. Hell—he no longer owns this town lock, stock and barrel."

As the days to the filing deadline had approached, Dak had spent sleepless nights, wrestling with the decision of whether or not to enter the mayor's race. As he and Kathy had rekindled their high school romance, the situation of the mayor's race had taken on more and more personal dimensions. That first day when he had come face-to-face with Kathy he had been overwhelmed with conflicting emotions. Her callous brush-off ten years ago had almost been too much for him to bear, and now the wound had opened, festering anew. But then at the reunion she'd insisted she had never known about his attempts to write and call, and he was inclined to believe her. Burke Ayers must have confiscated the letters, increasing Dak's bitterness toward her father.

Then came the moonlit night at his ranch when he kissed Kathy. He got that old feeling—strong as ever.

Suddenly the bid for mayor became a very personal issue. He thought about Kathy's temper. When she found out he had entered the race, she would be mad as a hornet. At the last minute, he'd made his decision. He decided to run anyway. It wouldn't be the first time Kathy had been mad at him.

Once the decision was made, Dak put all his energy into the race. The night before his first public speech, he and Cliff Dunlap discussed campaign strategy.

"The thing you have to keep pounding away at in this speech—in all your speeches—is the need for change," said his campaign manager. "I think we'll make that our campaign slogan—'Time For A Change in Endless.' The voters will get the idea."

"Did you see today's paper? The *Courier* came out with a strong editorial endorsing Kathy. The paper called me a glamour boy from California looking for local publicity. Not very complimentary."

"Well, you'll have to expect that kind of thing. It's no surprise to any of us that the one newspaper in town would support Kathy. Burke Ayers owns most of the media. We're not going to get any support from that corner, you can be sure of that! One thing we do have going for us is the fact that Kathy is a woman. It's still tough for a woman to be elected mayor, and doubly hard in a town like Endless. Some of the old-timers might vote against her just out of prejudice.''

''Well, we're not going to make that an issue in the campaign!'' Dak said heatedly. ''I'll drop out, first.''

''I didn't say we would,'' Cliff replied. ''I feel the same as you. I'm just stating a fact of life. Kathy has the support of the media and the political clout of her father. That's a big hill for you to climb. On your side, you've got a lot of the younger crowd and, like it or not, there is that prejudice that will swing votes against Kathy.''

''Maybe that's true, but I don't want to win the election because I'm a man. That's like having the devil in my corner.''

''I agree. Maybe you can make bring that out in your speech—that you don't want the matter of gender to enter into the race.''

''I intend to,'' Dak agreed, ''although I don't feel that I'm running against Kathy Ayers in the first place. It's her father I'm running against.''

The next day, shortly before noon, Dak entered the crowded dining room of the Steak House on main street. The members of the Civitan Club gathered at the tables represented the business and professional community.

At the speakers' table, Dak saw his opponents, Henry Jimpson and Kathy Ayers. Henry was a plump, middle-aged balding man with a round, affable face. He was broadcasting smiles and nods to the many familiar faces around the room. Next to him sat Kathy. Dak felt his pulse quicken at the sight of her. She looked smart and efficient—and to him, desirable—in a ruffled white blouse, high heels and a tailored gray suit that hugged her slender waist and trim hips. Wearing horn-rimmed reading glasses, she was frowning intently at a handful of notes. The glasses somehow made her look even sexier. Dak felt a strong primitive urge to take her in his arms and kiss the intent frown away.

The fantasy had his blood pounding as he took his place at the speakers' table. Kathy looked up and glared at him through her glasses. When he flashed her a wide grin, she flushed and jerked her gaze away, looking ahead.

Dak glanced over the crowd. Most of these people he had known since childhood. Local ranchers and farmers mingled with the bankers and merchants, and Dak spotted Burke Ayers at a distant table. The large, husky rancher was looking straight at him. For a moment, their eyes met. Anger burned like a red-hot coal in the pit of Dak's stomach and his jaw knotted fiercely.

The meeting of the Civitan Club came to order. After a reading of minutes and a brief discussion of

business matters lunch was served. As desserts were
finished, the chairman rose and introduced the day's
program—the kick-off of the mayoral race with each
candidate allowed a ten-minute speech outlining his
or her qualifications and platform.

Henry Jimpson was the first speaker. He gave a
short speech sprinkled with humorous anecdotes and
ended by saying, "Heck, I don't have to go on about
myself for you folks. You all know me. I've been
doin' a good job for you as mayor for the past ten
years. These two young people runnin' against me
are real nice kids. We've seen them grow up here. But
why should you go voting for an inexperienced
youngster when you got good old Henry Jimpson
with ten years' experience who can go right on bein'
the kind of mayor you've been comfortable with for
so long?"

Bowing in appreciation of friendly applause, the
mayor sat down.

Kathy was next to stand at the speaker's podium.
Her address was sharp, serious and businesslike, a
complete change from Jimpson's good-natured kidding. In a clear, concise voice, she outlined her edu-
cational and legal background. "This election is very
important to Endless," she said, her voice sounding
clear in the quiet room. "The town cannot go on
with its head in the sand. We're faced with some

problems that have been swept under the rug for years and they're going to become acute if we don't do something about them. Our water treatment plant is dangerously outdated. Streets are deteriorating. We need a new city hall and a library. Only a city administration with energy, vision and courage can tackle these problems. If you vote for me you'll get that kind of leadership. Your other choices are for the business-as-usual incumbent or for a newcomer, an outsider who is not in touch with the problems of our city and is not capable of dealing with them.''

The applause that followed her speech was loud and enthusiastic. She glared briefly at Dak as she sat down. He responded with a wry smile.

Dak took his place before the microphone. His experience in television had given him a polish he hadn't had when he'd left Endless ten years ago. Those who remembered him as a bronzed, wholesome but shy and inarticulate youngster were surprised at the confident, poised man who addressed them now. He had a stage presence that immediately captured and held the attention of the room.

''Back in the 1920s,'' Dak began, ''Texas had a governor named Jim Ferguson. Jim was a popular governor, but he got in a sticky political situation and had to resign under a threat of impeachment. Now, Mr. Ferguson wasn't one to give up power that easily. He had his wife, Miriam Ferguson, run for governor in his place and she got elected, Texas's first woman governor, back some forty or fifty years before anybody heard of the women's liberation movement. Texans called her 'Ma' Ferguson, and they voted for her with tongue-in-cheek because they knew good and well that she was a figurehead and they were really voting for Jim Ferguson, the power behind the throne. Today, we've got a situation something like that here in Endless. For the past ten years, Henry Jimpson has been your mayor, but it's common knowledge that it was the political backing of one of our prominent ranchers that put him in office and kept him there. Henry didn't make a move without first consulting that rancher. Now that same rancher's daughter is seeking the office. The question facing voters is this. Do you want that rancher to continue running your city? Because if you vote his daughter into office, you can be sure he'll be the power behind the throne just like Jim Ferguson. Ladies and gentlemen, I don't feel for one minute that I am running against Kathy Ayers in this election. I am running against her father, Burke Ayers!''

There was a rumble of surprised reaction in the room. Dak saw the hard, piercing eyes of Burke Ayers, blue and cold as steel, fastened on him. As he paused for a swallow of water, Dak saw Kathy out of the corner of his eye. She had never looked madder.

Dak finished his speech. "My opponent has inferred that I am an outsider who lacks the experience to fill the office. I want to respond to both of those accusations. Number one, all of you know I am no outsider. I grew up in Endless and graduated from school here. Everyone here knows me. It's true I've been away for ten years, but I'm back to stay. I own property here. I intend for my son to grow up here. As for my ability, I owned a large business with a dozen franchises in California and I was on the city council of the town where I lived. I know how to deal with the problems of this town in a businesslike and efficient manner. I'll appreciate your vote in this election. Thank you."

Dak sat down to scattered applause. Most appeared too stunned to react one way or another. Some were looking uneasily from Dak to Burke. The applause appeared to come from the younger businessmen.

Sam Trobridge, manager of a local computer and electronic store, leaned over to the person sitting next to him and murmured, "Wow. And I thought this was going to be a dull election!"

As the meeting broke up, Dak passed by Kathy who was gathering up her purse and notes. She was trembling with rage. Through her teeth, she said, "Dak Roberts, go to hell!"

He laughed. "I'm sure glad the paper can't quote you on that!"

"Even hell would be better off without a polecat like you!"

"You don't really mean that. How about having dinner with me tonight?"

"Only if I could serve you rat poison!"

With that, she turned her back on him and strode out of the room.

Kathy went straight from the luncheon to her office. Shortly after she sat down, her father came strolling in. He went straight to a liquor cabinet that Kathy kept stocked mainly for him, poured a generous amount of sour-mash bourbon into a tumbler, diluted it with just a splash of branch water, dropped a couple of ice cubes in the potent drink and then lowered himself into a chair and propped his boots on her desk. "Quite a speech young Roberts made," he observed, taking a long swallow.

Kathy was too agitated to stay seated and rose to stand with the picture window behind her. "We'll sue him! You have a perfect case, Daddy. Defamation of character. Libel. Invasion of privacy. Assault with a deadly weapon."

Burke Ayers raised a shaggy eyebrow. "Assault with a deadly weapon?"

"Yes—his mouth!"

Ayers chuckled. He swirled his drink, rattling the ice cubes.

"I'm serious! Sue him!"

Ayers's hard blue eyes studied her thoughtfully. "Honey, if everybody running for office in a Texas election filed a lawsuit because his opponent insulted him, the civil courts would be overworked for the next hundred years. Mudslinging is a tradition in Texas elections. You ought to know that by now. An election doesn't get to be any fun until the politicians can get down to calling each other names. Can't let things like that get to you if you're going to run for office."

"I wouldn't be so upset if he'd slung mud at me— inferred that I was a crook or couldn't handle the job. I'd just laugh it off. But the gall of Dak Roberts, standing up there and telling the whole town that if I get elected, you'd be running the town was really hitting below the belt."

"Well, honey, I wouldn't take him too seriously. You've got the voters solidly behind you. That boy doesn't stand a chance. Let him shoot off his mouth."

Kathy sat behind her desk, giving her father a penetrating look. "You sound awfully sure."

Burke shrugged. "Just stating facts."

She was still eyeing him critically. "You're not going back on your promise to keep out of politics and let me run my own campaign, are you?"

"What makes you say that?"

"You sound so smug, as if you know I've got the election wrapped up. And there's that editorial Sam Wilkie ran in his newspaper this week. I know you have controlling interest in the *Courier*. Sam works for you."

"That may be so, but I had nothing to do with Sam's endorsement. That was his idea. You know I leave the running of the newspaper strictly up to him."

Kathy was half convinced, but she still looked troubled. "Dak said some things to me a few days ago that made me mad at the time, but I've gotten to thinking about them since then and it started me wondering. He said he thought you'd influenced my decision to run for mayor. I denied it, but afterward I thought about it and I remembered that you first brought it up last Thanksgiving when I had you over to my place for a turkey dinner. You said Henry Jimpson was getting to be an old stick-in-the-mud and Endless needed some new blood in the mayor's office. Then at Christmas you asked me if I'd ever given any thought to holding public office. I laughed off the idea at the time, but you brought it up several times and got me to thinking about it.''

"I didn't twist your arm," Burke pointed out. "I found out a long time ago you've got a mind of your own. You made the decision to run."

"Yeah, but you put the idea in my head. Maybe Dak is partly right—maybe you do still influence me more than I realize."

Burke shrugged, downing the last of his drink. "I doubt it."

"Well, I just want us to be sure we understand each other. You're my daddy and I love you, but I know you like to throw your weight around. I don't want you twisting any arms in this election and if I do get to be mayor, I'm running things my way. I'm not going to go running to you for advice the way Henry Jimpson has done for the past ten years."

"Fair enough. You wouldn't listen to any advice I gave you anyway. Does this mean I don't get a turkey dinner next Thanksgiving?"'

Kathy laughed. She came around the table, sat on his lap and ruffled his hair. "You big old bear. No wonder you've got everybody in the county afraid of you. They don't know your bark is worse than your

bite, the way I do. You're just a big old pussycat.''
She kissed his forehead.

Burke chuckled, a deep rumble in his throat. He
patted her fondly. ''Where you're concerned I am,
little squirt. You might be a big lady lawyer and next
mayor of the town, but to me you're still a freckle-
faced little girl in pigtails like you were when I put
you on your first horse.''

Chapter Nine

After his speech at the Civitan Club luncheon, Kathy wanted to keep as much distance as possible between herself and Dak Roberts. Once again he had aroused her dreams only to crush them. She wanted nothing more to do with him, but she had promised Joedy that she would watch him perform in the children's rodeo. A strong bond had grown between her and the boy. She couldn't bear to let him down, so she decided to go.

The following Saturday, she drove to the ranch where the children's rodeo was being held, sponsored by the Kiwanis Club as a fund-raising event to benefit the cerebral palsy fund.

Kathy parked her car on the dusty grounds and walked around behind the chutes where the young contestants had gathered. When he spied her coming toward him, Joedy ran to meet her.

"Hi, cowboy." Her grin slashed her tan face.

"I was hoping you'd come."

"I promised you I'd be here to root for you, didn't I? Are you all ready to win first place?"

"I hope so," he said fervently. "The first-place trophy is a great saddle. Second place is a silver belt buckle." He looked excited and nervous.

Kathy turned him around to read the number pinned on his back. "Eight. Hey, that's your age!"

Junior Gomez, holding the reins of Joedy's horse, came over to join them. *"Buenos días, señorita,"* he said politely, tipping his hat.

"Buenos días. ¿Cómo estás, Junior?"

"Muy bien, gracias. ¿Y Usted?"

"Muy bien." Continuing to talk in Spanish, she asked, "Is Joedy's horse well trained?"

"Sí, señorita, I trained the *caballo* myself." He grinned. "In the barrel race, the *muchacho* has only to sit in the saddle. The horse knows what to do."

Kathy put her arm around Joedy's shoulder and walked with him to where the horses were being lined up for the opening event.

"I'll be in the stands rooting for you, cowboy," she promised.

"Thanks," Joedy said. "I'll do my best."

His freckles appeared more pronounced on his face that paled from nervous tension.

The show steward who was in charge of the event shouted orders for the riders to mount up for the opening parade through the arena. Kathy saw young riders of both sexes competing in Joedy's class. She squeezed his hand, then moved away in the direction of the bleachers. As she turned, she saw Dak striding toward his son. The sight of his broad-shouldered figure brought a rush of blood to her cheeks. She quickly looked away, pretending not to see him. At the concession stand she bought a bag of popcorn and a Coke, then she hurried to find a seat among the spectators. Someone clambered up the row of bleachers and sat beside her.

"Morning, Kathy," Dak greeted her.

She looked away without replying.

"It was nice of you to come. It means a lot to Joedy. He was counting on your being here."

"I promised him I'd come," she replied coldly. "I had no intention of letting him down."

Dak was silent for a moment. "I thought we were going to make the election a friendly race," he said after a while. "You don't sound very friendly."

"I don't feel very friendly," she responded, turning back to him, her eyes flashing angrily. "That speech of yours ended any friendship we might have had."

"I didn't say anything about my reason for getting in the race that you didn't already know."

"Yeah, but you said it in public."

"I didn't have any choice, Kathy. The only reason is to end your father's political control of the town. I had to make my position clear."

"You made it clear enough and insulted me doing it. You stood up there before the whole town and insinuated that I don't have a mind of my own, that I'm depending on my father to get me elected and when I'm mayor I'll be running to Daddy. Dak, I'll never forgive you for that."

"Well, you can prove I'm wrong easily enough if your father doesn't interfere in the election."

"He's not going to! I told him to butt out, that this is my campaign and if I'm elected it's going to be on my own efforts."

"Good for you."

"Yeah, but you've messed things up with your speech. You planted the notion in everybody's head that Daddy's going to use his influence to get me elected. Who's going to believe me now when I say he isn't?"

"If I see that he really is staying out of this election, I'll tell the voters so. I'll make a speech giving you credit and admit I was wrong about you and your father. Coming from me, they'll believe it."

She looked at him critically. "You'll do that?"

"I promise. But you have to convince me."

"I'll convince you all right. You'll see that Daddy's going to stay strictly out of my campaign."

"Okay. Now that that's settled, can we be friendly rivals?" Dak held out a hand.

Part of her wanted to tell him to jump in the lake, but his eyes were gazing straight into hers with the kind of intense intimacy that had always demoralized her. Berating her own weakness, she allowed him to take her hand and give it a squeeze.

Then the announcer's voice interrupted them. Kathy directed her attention to the ring.

The rodeo began with the young contestants on horseback galloping into the arena. They held the flag of the United States, the Lone Star flag of Texas, and the Kiwanis Club flag. The flags snapped colorfully as the dirt flew from under the galloping hooves.

The first event was a goat-tying contest. A goat was released from a chute and the young rider chased him on his horse, jumped down, captured the goat and tied him with a three-way hitch. It was a variation of the calf-roping contests popular with older teens and adult riders. Goat tying was considered a safer sport for the younger riders.

Kathy sat on the edge of her seat. Beside her, she felt Dak stiffen. The first contestant was a girl with brown pigtails. She did well, tying her goat in a matter of seconds as the spectators shouted encouragement. She was followed by a boy who took a bit longer. Then the announcer said, "Our next contestant in the goat-tying event is number eight, Joedy Roberts."

A chute door opened. Out ran the goat, and Joedy was after him instantly, urging Stampede on. He jumped down and in a flash had the goat tied.

Kathy was on her feet, along with the rest of the crowd, yelling at the top of her lungs. In the announcer's booth a timekeeper had his eye on the clock. The announcer's excited voice, sounding metallic over the loudspeakers, reported Joedy's time, the shortest so far. Kathy clapped excitedly.

The next event was the barrel race. When Joedy's turn came, Kathy saw that Junior Gomez had, indeed, trained Stampede well. The little cow pony made fast, expert turns around the barrels.

Several more events were on the program. There was a calf roundup where a half dozen kids on horseback chased calves around the ring, each con-

testant's goal to herd his designated calf into a chute.
In an egg race, the contestant was handed a raw egg
to balance on a spoon. Holding the spoon, he was to
circle the arena on horseback as fast as possible. If
he dropped the egg, he was disqualified. Last on the
program was calf riding. The youngster was given a
young calf, a yearling, to try to ride. The timekeeper
clocked the ride from the moment the boy climbed
on the colt's back until he hit the ground.

Kathy thought Joedy did well in all the events except the egg race. She held her breath while the
judges totaled the scores. After an interminable de-
lay, the announcer pronounced a boy named Tom
Estes the first-place winner and now the proud owner
of the trophy saddle. Then the announcer said,
"Second place, winner of the silver buckle, is Joedy
Roberts."

Kathy jumped up and down with excitement. She
felt Dak's arms around her and hugged him back
impulsively, forgetting for the moment that she de-
spised him.

Proud tears shone in his eyes. "That's my boy!"
Dak said, grinning from ear to ear. At that moment,
it was hard for her to remember they were enemies.

They hurried from the stand to where Junior was
helping Joedy down from his horse. The winners
were gathering in a group where the Kiwanis

president was awarding the prizes, which had been donated by a local feed store. Cameras flashed. Parents and friends crowded around the group.

Joedy saw Dak and Kathy and ran to them, proudly showing off his trophy—the ornate silver buckle engraved with the name of the event and the date. "They're going to have my name put on it next week," he exclaimed.

Dak laughed, grabbing the boy and swinging him up on his shoulder. Everybody was laughing and talking at once. Kathy reached up to squeeze Joedy's hand.

"Did you see me, Kathy?"

"Of course. Didn't you hear me yelling? I think I strained a vocal chord!"

"I didn't hear anything. I was scared I was going to mess up somewhere. I dropped the egg, but I guess I did okay on everything else."

"Well, rodeo star, I think this calls for a celebration," Dak exclaimed. "How about a poolside party tonight?"

"Great!" Joedy cried, his eyes sparkling. "Will you come, Kathy?"

"I—I don't know—"

"Please come," Dak said, looking straight at her. "Joedy would be disappointed if you didn't."

"I sure would!" Joedy insisted. "It wouldn't be a party without you, Kathy."

"Well, all right then."

"Everybody in swimsuits," Dak said. "We'll lounge around the pool and swim and eat barbecue and ice cream."

That afternoon Kathy went shopping for a new bathing suit. She selected a white maillot with a flowered detachable skirt.

Shortly before sundown, Kathy drove to Dak's ranch. When she arrived, she saw that Dak had decorated the patio with balloons and jack-o'-lanterns. The delicious aroma of mesquite smoke from a barbecue pit filled the air.

Joedy scrambled out of the pool and ran up to her. "Come in for a swim, Kathy!" he cried, tugging at her hand.

"Okay," she said with a grin. Now she kicked off her sandals, and started to remove the shirt and jeans she had thrown on over her suit. Suddenly, she became aware of Dak on the opposite side of the pool, gazing at her. A hot flush colored her cheeks as she realized that it looked as if she were undressing in front of him. Hurriedly, she finished stripping the blue jeans from her legs, dancing on one foot as the denim got tangled around an ankle. Then she was free of them and made a quick dive, welcoming the cool water on her hot skin.

She romped in the water with Joedy for a while before Dak joined them with a rubber ball for a game of keep-away. Once, when scrambling for the ball, Kathy became tangled in Dak's arms. For a heart-pounding moment, his hard, slick body moved against her bare flesh. Unnerved, she fought the water to get away.

After tiring themselves out, they clambered out of the pool and stretched out in reclining chairs. Kathy dried her hair with a towel Dak provided, then snapped on her skirt, arranging it to cover her legs. Dak brought them plates heaped with tender barbe-cue, crisp salad and pinto beans.

It was a pleasant, warm Texas evening with a gentle Gulf breeze wafting across the prairie. Over-head, stars sparkled in the black velvet sky. Junior Gomez brought his guitar from the bunkhouse and entertained them, singing melodious, sentimental Spanish ballads.

By ten o'clock, exhausted from the day's activi-ties and filled with barbecue and ice cream, Joedy was falling asleep in his chair. Dak sent him off to bed.

Conscious of not wanting to be alone with Dak, Kathy quickly gathered up her belongings. "Time I trundle off to bed, too."

"Thank you for coming, Kathy. It meant a lot to Joedy."

She nodded. "I enjoyed being with him. He's a great little kid."

"I enjoyed being with you," Dak said, looking at her directly. "For once we weren't at each other's throats."

"Only a temporary truce, for Joedy's sake," she said, her voice cool. "Don't get the idea I've changed my opinion of you."

He ignored the verbal jab. "Don't rush off. Have one more swim with me—for old time's sake."

"Don't start that old-time's-sake jazz with me again," she said, her cheeks coloring. "That's what got me in trouble the last time I was alone with you in the moonlight."

He chuckled, his eyes laughing...appealing. He looked up at the sky. "No moon tonight, just stars. You're safe." Lazily, he rose from his lounge chair and took her hand. "Come on. Remember how we used to race. You beat me sometimes."

His hand clasped hers strongly...too strongly. "You let me win," she said, aware that her voice had thickened.

"Don't be too sure about that. You were good, Kathy. You might have been Olympic material yourself, if you'd worked at it."

"That was ten years ago. I've spent a lot of time behind a desk since then. I'm out of shape."

A lazy, tantalizing grin spread over his tanned features as his gaze ranged the length of her figure, lingering over her breasts and slender hips. "I'd say you are in pretty good shape."

Burning heat warmed her flesh again. "Don't say that," she said unsteadily.

"How about that swim?"

"Well . . . just a short one."

She nervously unzipped the sarong, glaring at him. "Will you stop looking at me as if I'm doing a strip-tease?"

"Sorry. Hard not to enjoy the view, though. You have beautiful legs, Kathy."

Instead of replying, she dove into the pool.

There was a splash behind her as Dak split the water in a smooth, expert dive. Kathy swam quickly to the opposite side of the pool. Dak followed, stopping a few feet from her.

With her back against the tiled side, she balanced herself with her elbows resting on the gutter. The water slapped softly against the edge of the pool. She looked at Dak and could tell by the light in his eyes that he wanted to kiss her.

"Keep your distance," she warned nervously.

Instead, he moved closer, until he was just inches away. He looked into her eyes, then his gaze drifted down her face to her wet, glistening shoulders and the rounded curves of her breasts just above the water's edge. "That's not easy to do," he said softly. "Pretty girl, beautiful night."

She felt cornered as Dak moved closer. His lips brushed hers; her body drifted against his. She felt his thigh move sensuously against her leg. Her breath caught. "Dak, don't start this," she said unevenly.

"Why not? You want me to kiss you. I can see it in your eyes."

"No, I don't."

"Would you say that under oath?" he teased.

She avoided his eyes. "There's no point in it, Dak. There's no point at all in stirring up these old feelings."

Again his lips touched hers. She felt her mouth yield under his as a shudder of desire went through her. She pulled back. "You're not making this any easier for me," she said angrily.

"I really don't want to. Why should I?"

"No reason from your standpoint," she agreed. "You know what happens when I let you kiss me. I stop using my brain. That's just what you want, isn't it?''

"What I want, Kathy," he said huskily, "is to hold you close, to kiss you, to feel you responding..."

She suddenly ducked under his arm. In a flash, she swam half the length of the pool underwater. Then she surfaced and continued swimming with hard strokes. Dak was close behind, churning the water. She reached the far end and started dragging herself out of the water, but Dak grabbed at her waist, pulling her back in. They were both laughing and breathless.

"I said you were good," Dak said between gasps for breath. "You stayed ahead of me the length of the pool."

"I'm paying for it now,"she panted. "Told you I was out of shape."

They were standing at the shallow end in waist-deep water. Dak took in her glistening, bare shoulders, watched her breasts rising and falling as she gasped for breath. Hunger for her was coursing through his blood in heated waves.

He pulled her close, holding her until she had her breath back, then he drew her with him, swimming slowly to deeper water. She was too spent to struggle free.

Dak stopped, letting their feet drift down to the pool floor. The water was up to Kathy's neck.

He held her against him. She felt his body against hers, her bare leg caught between his thighs, her wet cheek pressed against her shoulder, her eyes closed. "I wish you wouldn't do this to me," she said hopelessly.

His palms were moving over her bare back, down to her waist, over the curves of her hips, foraging a sensual trail over her heated flesh.

"Dak," she said thickly, "this is just going to make me miserable."

"I don't see why."

He was slipping the top of her suit from her shoulders. "Kathy, nothing has changed between us. We're taking up where we left off ten years ago."

"Things are not the same. Back then I was a silly high school girl in love with love."

"I don't believe that. It must have been more than that. The feeling is still there between us, as strong as ever."

He had pulled her suit down, freeing her breasts. He caressed their delicate wet curves under the water, then pulled her close. She felt the texture of the hair on his hard chest against her breasts and moaned softly, her eyes closed.

With a shudder, she drew back abruptly, pulling the straps of her suit back over her shoulders. She was breathing almost as hard as when they'd raced. "All right, you've proved your point. You could seduce me without much trouble. A few more kisses and you'll probably be able to take me up to bed with you. Where does that leave me tomorrow?"

"Kathy, this isn't just a fling—"

"It very well could be. You've been a widower for a year. You need a woman. You run into an old girlfriend from high school days. Why not take advantage of the situation? What have you got to lose?"

He cupped her face in his hands, forcing her to gaze into his eyes. "It isn't like that, Kathy. I wouldn't do that to you."

"I don't trust you," she said raggedly. "I don't know what you're going to say about me or my father in public next. You have a way of jerking the rug out from under me. You got mad at me and took off for California, breaking my heart. Maybe you did plan to send for me. I don't know what to believe. Then you come back here, get a lot of old hopes stirred up, and then out of the blue announce that you're running against me for mayor. You make a speech before the whole town, insulting me and my father. You have some kind of grudge against my father and he apparently feels the same about you.

I'm supposed to sleep with you under these circumstances?'' She shook her head, backing away from him and climbing out of the pool. Grabbing up her belongings, she ran to her car before Dak could touch her again.

Chapter Ten

During the following weeks, Endless took on the appearance of a town in the grip of a hotly contended mayoral race. Two large red, white and blue billboards with Kathy's picture exclaimed Kathy's The One For Us! Fences and posts all over town were festooned with posters put out by the three candidates. Ayers, Roberts and Jimpson bumper stickers were plastered on cars. Numerous political rallies were held weekly.

Kathy threw herself into her campaign with every ounce of her energy, shaking hands at the malls, attending rallies, making television commercials and public speeches.

A meeting was held in her office one night to assess how well her campaign was going. Present were Arthur Peters; her publicity chairman Fred Turner; and Jack Newhart, the head of her fund-raising committee.

Brice Williams had brought Kathy to the meeting.

"Money isn't a problem," Jack Newhart said. "You've got the banking and ranching community solidly behind you, Kathy, and most of the older, established businesses. We can afford all the billboards, TV spots and newspaper ads we need to swamp Dak Roberts's campaign. I understand they're having a struggle to raise funds. Our ads are running two to one of theirs."

Arthur Peters was less enthusiastic. "I'm not sure how much good all that media advertising does in a town this size. It's the personal contact that counts, the hand shaking, baby kissing, grass-roots electioneering, and Dak seems to be pretty good at that. I had some people run a straw poll, and it looks like you and Dak are running neck and neck, Kathy. If I were a betting man, I wouldn't give odds either way."

Kathy pressed her lips together angrily. "I don't see how people can let that man pull the wool over their eyes that way. How is he convincing them he'd make such a great mayor?"

"People vote for emotional reasons," her campaign manager replied. "They like Dak. He's a local hero. He's got lots of charm, lots of charisma."

"What am I—the bride of Frankenstein?"

"Not at all. People like and respect you, Kathy. There's just something a bit more glamorous about Dak. And remember, you're also battling prejudice. Any time a woman runs for mayor she's got to cut through that barrier. Dallas and Houston have elected women, proving that it can be done, but in some smaller, conservative communities, it's still a tough fight. You'll make history around here if you get elected, Kathy."

"I don't want to make history," she said glumly. "I just want to give Endless the kind of mayor it needs to handle the problems it's facing. I don't know if Dak can do that, I don't care how much charisma he has." Then she asked, "How about this issue of my father?"

"Hard to say for sure," Peters admitted. "I think it's gotten him some votes among the younger crowd, but it's also made him some enemies among the older, established businessmen who are friends of your father."

They discussed campaign strategy for the final weeks of the campaign, then Brice took Kathy to dinner.

They made small talk during the meal. Over dessert and coffee, Brice ventured, "This campaign is really getting to you, Kathy, isn't it?"

"What do you mean?"

"I've never seen you so intense over anything before. You've been running yourself ragged since the campaign began. There are circles under your eyes. You've lost weight."

"Well, it's important, Brice. You know the outcome of this election can affect the future of this community for years to come."

Brice leaned back in his chair, sipping his coffee, giving her a searching look. "I know all about that. But you weren't this worked up when you thought you were just running against Jimpson."

"I didn't think Henry had much of a chance. With Dak Roberts it's different. He could very well win this election."

"Yes," Brice said, nodding slowly. "I'm sure Dak makes the difference. Is it something personal now, Kathy?"

She looked at him sharply. "What do you mean by that?"

He smiled wryly. "Kathy, I know you've been carrying a torch for Dak ever since high school. Now he's back and the two of you are running against each other in a hot local election. Don't tell me all this hasn't got personal overtones.''

"Dak made it personal when he publicly attacked my father and insinuated that I couldn't get elected without Dad's help!''

"Sure that's all?''

"Of course. What else should there be?''

"I don't know, frankly. Maybe that's what I'm trying to find out. You know how I feel about you, Kathy; how I've felt for years. I kept hoping someday you'd want my engagement ring again. But then Dak came back. I've kind of been watching from the sidelines to see if the two of you would get together again. I was really surprised when Dak announced he was running against you for mayor.''

"No more surprised than I was,'' she said grimly.

Brice was silent for a moment. "That doesn't answer my question, though. The election aside, how are things between you and Dak? Personally, I mean? Dak is a widower. You're single. Are you going to take up where you left off?''

Kathy's eyes were clouded. "I don't know, Brice. Dak is a complex person. I'm not sure if he ever was really in love with me. He's been having a lot of trouble with his son since the boy's mother died. Joedy has taken a liking to me. Somehow I've been able to bring him out of his shell. That was impor-

tant to Dak. Maybe that's all I mean to him now—
someone to help raise Joedy. Dak says he still cares
for me in the old way, but I don't see how I can believe him. How could he care for me, then challenge
me in this race just out of spite toward my father?
That's something else about Dak that I don't understand—the bitterness and antagonism he feels toward my father. He thinks Daddy broke us up when
we were teenagers. I can understand his being mad
about that, but it seems to be more than that—''

Brice nodded. ''Of course there is. You mean you
don't know?''

''Know what?''

''That your father and Dak's father were rivals for
the same woman.''

Kathy's eyes widened with surprise. ''Dak's
mother?'' she gasped.

Brice nodded. ''You know my dad is an old
ranching buddy of your father. He told me the story
a long time ago. Dak's mother was the prettiest girl
in the county. Your father was courting her. They
were engaged until Dak's father moved into town,
swept her off her feet, and they eloped. It broke
Burke Ayers's heart. He never got over it. He never
forgave them. He fixed it so Dak's father couldn't get
a bank loan or get credit with the farm-implement
stores. Burke could do that—he was chief stock-

holder at the bank and had a lot of influence with the local merchants. Without the money to buy farm machinery, Dak's family stayed poor."

Kathy paled, numb with shock. Now she understood a lot of things that had puzzled her before. Dak's intense bitterness and her parents' failed marriage. On the one hand, she felt a wave of pity and sorrow for the heartbreak her father had kept to himself all these years. On the other hand, she was angry and disillusioned.

"You'd better take me home, Brice," she said. She wanted to be alone, to sort out her thoughts, to come to terms with this unexpected revelation.

It was early one morning in the final two weeks of the campaign that Dak was awakened by loud knocking at his front door. Dak had made a speech at a political rally the night before and had gotten to bed late. He looked at his watch groggily. Puzzled, he groped for his robe and walked yawning to the front door where, to his surprise, he saw Cliff Dunlap.

His campaign manager wore a grim expression as he entered the house. "Have you seen this morning's paper?" he blurted out.

"Are you kidding? I got to bed after one o'clock last night. No, I haven't seen the morning paper."

Dunlap opened the paper he was carrying and pointed to a story on the front page.

Political Scandal Haunts Mayoral Candidate.

Dak Roberts, candidate for mayor of Endless, has a political record tinged with scandal, the *Courier* learned late yesterday. While living in California, Roberts was elected to a city council that was recalled under a cloud of criminal charges. Several council members were indicted by the grand jury....

Dak stared unbelievingly at the article. He felt stunned, unable for a moment to react. Then he angrily crumpled the paper.

Cliff Dunlap paced the room in agitation. "Dak, is the story true?"

Dak trembled with rage. "It's true that the city council I was on was recalled," he said through tight lips. "Some of the council members were accepting bribes to award construction contracts. I was not involved. I just happened to have had the bad luck to be a member of the council at the time. The voters recalled the entire council to wipe the slate clean, but this story neglects to mention that I was never charged with any criminal activity. This is slanted to make it sound as if everyone on the council was a crook, including me. This doesn't come right out and say I was a crook, but anyone reading it would think so."

"I'm not surprised," Dunlap said. "The *Courier* has made no bones about being behind Kathy Ayers from the beginning. Their editorial page and all their news stories are slanted against us."

"They must have gotten real worried about how the campaign was going and went to some extra lengths to dig this up," Dak muttered, still half-dazed. "They must have sent a reporter to California to see if he could find something in my past that could be used against me and he came up with this."

"Well, it's bad," Cliff exclaimed, his expression grim. "This could very well lose us the election. It won't help much for you to deny this. No matter how you try to set the record straight, you'll be tainted by it. Voters will read this and say, 'I'd better not vote for Roberts. He'll be dipping his fingers in the municipal cash register.'"

Dak's fury was growing by leaps and bounds. "I know who's behind this," he said, banging his right fist into his left palm. "Burke Ayers. He owns the newspaper, doesn't he?"

"He's the major stockholder," Cliff answered.

Dak nodded. "Just like he owns or runs everything else in Endless," Dak said bitterly. "Kathy almost had me believing that the old tyrant was staying out of this campaign, but I was right from the beginning. It explains a lot of things—why Kathy's campaign has gotten such large donations, for example. And this news story. Burke Ayers would do anything to defeat me. He got worried when he saw what a strong campaign I've been running. He ordered his stooges at the newspaper to smear me."

"It sounds possible," Cliff agreed.

"It's more than possible," Dak growled. He jumped up. In ten minutes he was dressed and in his pickup, driving furiously into town. He stormed into Kathy Ayers's office, brushed aside her receptionist and banged open the door to her inner office.

Kathy, who was speaking on the phone, looked up, her eyes wide with surprise. She hung up the phone and rose to her feet.

Dak threw the newspaper on her desk. "Have you seen this?"

She swallowed hard and nodded. "I was just on the phone, trying to get the editor of the *Courier*."

"Why? To thank him?"

She turned pale. "Of course not! How dare you say such a thing, Dak? I was calling him to demand an explanation."

"I'll give you an explanation," Dak raged, pacing the rug before her desk, trying to keep control of himself. "Your father decided I might win this election. He'd never stand for that, so he ordered his stooge down at the newspaper to indulge in a little yellow journalism. He's had a reporter snooping in my private life trying to dig up some dirt that would cost me some votes. They came up with this city council thing back in California and made it sound as if I were involved in the graft. Kathy, my only mistake was the misfortune of being on a city council with a bunch of crooks. I had absolutely nothing to do with the corruption. There was a grand jury investigation. They returned indictments against several council members, but I was completely cleared. The story in today's paper conveniently overlooked that fact. People reading it will see just the headline and read that I was involved in a political scandal back in California. It makes me look guilty as hell. Who would vote for me after reading something like this?"

Kathy nervously twisted a ring on one finger. Her face was pale. "Dak, I can't blame you for being furious. I also know why you're bitter toward my father—Brice told me about the feud. But I have trouble believing Daddy would stoop to something like this."

"Do you? Are you willing to believe he confiscated those letters I wrote you from California?"

"Yes, I think he might have done that. It's the kind of thing an overly protective parent might have done. You know my mother died when I was Joedy's age. My dad had to be both a mother and father to me. I guess that made him unreasonably protective. He was afraid I'd run off and marry you when I was too young to know my own mind. He'd have done anything to keep me from making a mistake that would mess up my whole life. But Dak, that was ten years ago. He was doing what he thought best for a teenage daughter. I'm a grown woman now. I don't believe he'd stoop to anything like that now."

"Don't be too sure, Kathy. Your father never forgave my father for winning the hand of the woman he loved. He'd die before he'd let a Roberts become mayor of Endless."

Kathy looked pale and shaken. "Dak," she said, "I just can't believe that's true. But I'm going to find out. If it is true, if my father arranged to have that story printed, then I'm going to withdraw from the race."

Kathy was emotionally torn up when she left her office that morning and drove to her father's ranch. She had been brooding about her father ever since Brice told her the story of the love triangle, and suspected that Dak might be right about her father secretly backing her campaign. Some of her biggest contributors were business associates of Burke Ayers. She tried not to believe that. Her father had promised to stay out of the campaign and she wanted to believe that he was a man of his word.

Now, with the story that appeared in this morning's newspaper, she could no longer bury her head in the sand. A confrontation with her father was unavoidable.

She found him in his office in the front of the big, rambling house. This was not only the headquarters of his ranching operation, but of his many business interests as well. He was behind a desk piled high with papers and books. His secretary, a middle-aged woman who had been with him for years, was going over the books with him. When Kathy walked into the room, Burke raised his head. He looked surprised. "Hi, sweetheart. What brings you out here on a weekday morning?"

"Good morning, Dad," she said. "Good morning, Mrs. Schultze." Her voice was strained. "Dad, I need to talk to you."

"Sure, honey. Why don't you bring those figures up to date, Mrs. Schultze? We'll finish these books this afternoon."

"Of course, Mr. Ayers."

The woman gathered up an armload of books and papers. Giving Kathy a parting smile, she left the room.

"You look kind of grim, Kathy," Burke said. Then he chuckled. "Is somebody suing me?"

Kathy sighed, sinking into a deep chair in front of his desk. "I wish it were that simple." She had brought a copy of the morning's paper. "Have you seen this?"

Burke shook his head. "Haven't had time to look at the paper this morning." He reached across the desk and took the paper she handed him.

There was silence in the room except for the steady swing of pendulum in an old-fashioned clock mounted on the wall. Kathy watched her father's face scowl darkly as he read the article about Dak Roberts. He tossed the paper on the desk. "Looks like Sam Wilkie kinda went overboard on that one. I don't like that kind of journalism."

"You don't?"

He looked at her curiously. "Of course not!"

"You can see how damaging this will be to Dak's campaign."

"Of course. They don't actually come out and say he was a crook, but the story implies that he was a part of a city council involved in some shady dealings."

"He had nothing to do with it. He innocently got elected to a city council that had some bad apples. When the scandal broke, some of the dirt rubbed off on him. He explained all that to me, and I believe him. Whatever other faults he may have, Dak is honest as the day is long. The grand jury cleared him, but the story doesn't make that clear."

Then Kathy gave her father a searching look. She drew a ragged breath. "Daddy, I want you to level with me. When this race started, I told you that you were not to interfere. Have you kept your promise?"

Anger flared in Burke's eyes. "Now see here, young lady—"

"All I want is a straight answer."

"I gave you my word. Are you questioning that?" he asked ominously.

"Things seem to have broken my way. I've gotten large contributions from businessmen who I know are your buddies. Now this story in the morning paper. You know this will kill any chance Dak has. You own controlling interest in the *Courier*. I just want to know if Sam Wilkie was acting on your orders when he dug up this story."

"It's a good thing you're my daughter," Burke growled. "If a man had come in here talking to me like that, somebody would have to carry him out."

"I'm sorry, but I have to know the truth. Daddy, I've found out some things that are very painful to me. I wish I didn't have to bring this up, but it explains why I'm so upset. Brice Williams told me a lot about you and Mr. Roberts. Now I understand why you've disliked Dak so violently all these years. He reminded you of his father."

Kathy winced at the look that crossed Burke's face. He turned pale and suddenly looked every bit of his sixty-eight years. Rising, he went to a cabinet and poured some bourbon into a glass. He swirled it around, looking at it absently, then drank it in a swallow. He put the glass down, walked to a window and looked out over his ranch, resting his fingertips on the sill. "Brice Williams has a big mouth," he said quietly, his voice tired.

Tears stung Kathy's eyes. "I'm glad he told me. It explains a lot of things. I wish you'd talked to me about it long ago, Daddy."

He was silent.

"Is that why you were so dead set against Dak and me before he went out to California?"

Burke shook his head. "Not altogether. I didn't fancy the idea of you getting hitched to Bill Roberts's son, but I wouldn't have interfered if you'd been older. I was afraid you were too young to know your own mind, that you were going to do something crazy like run off with the boy.''

"I have to know something. Dak told me that after he left he wrote letters and tried to call. I never got the letters or the phone messages. Did you intercept them?''

He didn't reply, but she heard him sigh, saw his shoulders sag. She had her answer.

In a moment, he turned. His voice sounded tired and old. ''Kathy, I hope one day you'll have children, my grandchildren. You'll find out when you do that being a good parent is the toughest job there is. You can go to school and learn how to be a doctor or a lawyer or a teacher. Or you can spend a few years learning a trade. I know all there is to know about raising cattle. I didn't know the first thing about raising a daughter. They don't teach you how to parent. One day you are handed this little human being to raise and you muddle along somehow. If you're lucky, you do a few things right. Mostly, it seems, you do a lot of things wrong. I spent many sleepless nights, worrying about you when you had that crush on Dak. I didn't think you were old enough to know your own mind. I wanted you to go to college, to make something of yourself. I didn't want you throwing it all away on an infatuation. I did what I thought was best for you at the time. Maybe it was one of those times I was wrong.''

Kathy swallowed a painful lump. "Do you still feel that way, Daddy? Do you think you have to protect me, do things for my best interest?''

He shook his head. "Of course not. You're a grown woman now.''

"Then tell me the truth about this story in the *Courier*.''

He looked directly into her eyes. "I had absolutely nothing to do with it. The first I heard about it was when you handed me the newspaper a few minutes ago. I gave you my word that I'd keep out of this race and I have.''

Kathy felt as if the weight of world had been lifted from her heart. The next moment she was in her father's arms, hugging him tightly.

Burke Ayers patted his daughter clumsily. He cleared his throat, then said, "Now I think I'd better go have a talk with Dak Roberts.''

Chapter Eleven

After confronting Kathy in her office, Dak had returned to his ranch. It was later that morning when Dak saw the pickup truck cross the cattle guard and pull up into his yard. He watched as the big man behind the wheel got out. With surprise, he recognized the driver. Burke Ayers was probably the last man in Texas that Dak expected to visit his ranch this morning.

Dak stepped down from the front porch of his house and stood waiting as Ayers approached him. He had not seen Kathy's father since the Civitan luncheon when Dak gave the first speech of his campaign. Now, as he watched the other man walking toward him, he was impressed again with the size of Burke Ayers. He was a big man—broad shouldered, barrel chested, with big, gnarled hands and a great shaggy head of white hair framing a face burned a dark mahogany by the sun and wind. The blue eyes that peered from under heavy white eyebrows were like chips of blue steel.

Ayers walked straight up to Dak. They stood there for a moment, the two tall men facing each other. Dak felt a lifetime of resentment toward this man welling up in him.

Ayers cleared his throat. "Dak, I came here to clear something up. Kathy brought this morning's *Courier* to me. She thought I had something to do with the story the paper ran about you today."

"Didn't you?"

Burke's cold blue eyes met Dak's unflinchingly. "Absolutely not. Kathy came to me when this mayor's race began and made me give her my word to keep out of it. I'm not a man who goes back on his word."

Dak had to admit that was true. Whatever his other sins might be, Burke Ayers was known to be a man of his word.

Ayers went on. "Kathy thought because I own an interest in the newspaper, I might have had something to do with getting Sam Wilkie to pry into your past and sling some mud. I assured her I had absolutely nothing to do with it. The first I heard about it was when she brought the paper to me this morning. I came here to tell you the same thing. I also want to make it completely clear to you that I have not lifted a finger on her behalf in this campaign."

Dak's reaction was mixed. He believed Burke Ayers was telling the truth. It could not have been easy for a man with his stubborn pride to drive over here. Dak was relieved for Kathy's sake. At the same time it was not easy to brush aside a lifetime of anger.

Several moments passed before Dak answered. Finally he said stiffly, "I appreciate your coming here to tell me this."

"Well, that's not the only reason I came," Ayers said, his voice rumbling in his deep chest. "There are other matters that need to be talked about. I think you know what I mean. There hasn't been any love lost between your father and me. I'm sure you feel the same."

"That's certainly true," Dak said coldly.

"I want you to know that if it weren't for Kathy, I wouldn't be here. This isn't easy for me, but my daughter is the only person who really matters to me in my life. When she started dating you, I thought it was no more than an infatuation that she'd get over.

I didn't think you had much of a future and I tried to break it up for her sake. I hoped she and Brice Williams would get together. But ten years have gone by and she never married. I've finally come to realize it was because she never got over you. When she drove out to my place this morning, coming to your defense over this newspaper thing, I could see in her eyes how much she still cares for you. I'm not going to ask you how you feel about her. You're both adults now and it's none of my business. But just in case the two of you should get together, I think things ought to be set straight between you and me."

Dak drew a breath, anger knotting his jaw. "How do you propose we do that?" he asked with a bitter edge in his voice. "How can a few words wipe out the memories I have of the look of defeat on my father's face when he came back from the bank after being turned down for a loan time and again? How can I forget the years of growing up poor, all because of you?"

Ayers sighed. "Words won't change a thing," he agreed. "It won't wipe out the past or the way you feel. I'm just thinking about Kathy. She knows now about what happened between me and your father. She knows how you hate me on account of it. What do you think this is going to do to her if the two of you get together? If we stay enemies, she's going to be torn between her love for you and her love for her daddy. I don't expect either one of us to forget the past, but for Kathy's sake I was hoping we could keep it in the past where it belongs.''

"That's not going to be easy."

"No, it isn't. A lot of it depends on how much you care for my girl and her happiness. I'm willing to meet you halfway.'' Ayers hesitated, then went on, "I know you think I made things tough for your father just to get even. It was more than that. Sometimes a man can love a woman so much, a lifetime isn't enough to get over her. That's how it was with me and your mother. She was so beautiful, it almost hurt me to look at her. Forty years have passed since the first day I saw her and it seems as if it were yesterday.'' He tapped his chest. "The feeling is still here, as strong as it was then, and the pain is just as bad. I never gave up hoping that maybe she'd come back to me, even after she married your father. That was why I did everything I could to keep him from making a go of his place—not to get even, but to try to get her back. I thought if she saw he was a failure, and saw how prosperous I was, she'd realize I could give her a much better life and she'd come back to me. A man can make an awful fool of himself over a woman and that's what I did. I threw away my own marriage to Kathy's mother because of her. It's taken me most of my life to finally face the truth—that your mother loved your father. Success or failure won't change a love like that. I'm telling you all this to get it out in the open, so maybe you'll understand things a little better."

Dak stared at Burke Ayers, the man who had cast a dark shadow over his life for so many years. He realized what it must have cost the old rancher to bare his innermost feelings like this. Cutting off an arm wouldn't have been more painful. Only his love for his daughter could have made him do this.

Slowly Dak nodded. "All right. For Kathy's sake, I agree it would be better to bury the hatchet. I can't change how I feel about you overnight. But maybe I can keep my feelings to myself. It makes it a little easier, knowing that I've been able to give my parents a comfortable place of their own now to make up for all the tough times. I'm willing to meet you halfway."

"That's all I ask," Burke said.

They were silent for a moment, sharing a look of agreement and a nod. For now, Dak thought, it would have to be as close as they could come to a handshake.

"Now I'd appreciate it if you'd come with me," Burke said abruptly. "I want to have a talk with Sam

Wilkie down at the paper, and I want you and Kathy present.''

Kathy was dumbfounded when her father and Dak walked into her office together. Before she could ask for an explanation, her father started talking. ''Kathy, I'm going over to have a talk with Sam Wilkie. I'd like you and Dak to go with me.''

She looked from her father to Dak, but could read nothing in their faces to explain what was going on. They left Kathy's office and walked together in silence across the street and down three blocks to the building that housed the town's newspaper. Burke looked grim and Dak was busy with his own thoughts.

The private office of the newspaper editor had glass walls on three sides so Sam Wilkie could look over the busy newsroom from his desk. Burke opened his door, ushered Kathy and Dak in and closed the door.

Wilkie rose, his face a study in surprise at the sight of the unlikely trio barging into his office.

'''Morning, Sam,'' Burke rumbled.

''Good morning, Burke.'' He nodded at the other two. ''Good morning Kathy, Dak.''

The gathering tension felt like a time bomb in the small office. Kathy looked at the three men. Wilkie, recovering from his first surprise, appeared to be growing uncomfortable. Dak's expression was stiff and reserved. Then she looked at her father and saw the hard glint of anger in his keen blue eyes.

Burke spread the crumpled morning paper he'd brought with him over Wilkie's desk. He stabbed the story about Dak with a heavy forefinger. "Sam, what got into you to print something like this?"

"What are you talking about, Burke? It's a good story."

"It's garbage! You took a few facts and distorted them to smear Dak Roberts's reputation. I hope he retains Kathy to sue the pants off you."

"Now hold on a minute, Burke," Wilkie blustered. "Don't come in here making threats like that. There isn't a word in that story that isn't true."

"Yeah, but you left out some of the truth— enough to distort the whole story. What you wound up with is an ugly bunch of half-truths, propaganda to assassinate Roberts's character and reputation."

"He was part of a city council that was so corrupt the voters held a recall election!"

"That didn't make me guilty of any crime," Dak said angrily. "The grand jury cleared me. You failed to make that clear."

Wilkie shrugged. "I can't help how readers interpret a story." He glared at Burke. "Why are you so upset? This could be what it takes to put Kathy in the mayor's office."

"I don't want to win the election with this kind of rotten journalism!" Kathy cried furiously.

"Well, excuse me! Burke, I thought I was doing you and Kathy a favor. The *Courier* has been behind her a hundred percent in this election. I figured you'd thank me."

"Is that why you've been pushing so hard to get her elected? Just to please me?" Burke demanded.

"Well, sure."

Burke looked at Kathy and Dak apologetically. "I'm sorry. I sure didn't encourage him." He directed his attention back to Wilkie. "I want you to run a story on page one of your next edition, clearing up this ugly mess. I want you to apologize to your readers for misleading them. I want you to make it crystal clear that Dak was an innocent victim of circumstance, that he had absolutely nothing to do with the corruption that went on in that city council."

"Now just a damn minute. I can't publish that kind of story."

"Can't or won't?"

"I won't. It would make me the laughing stock of the business. You might own the controlling interest in this paper, Burke, but I'm still the editor. I run this paper. You don't."

Burke leaned over the desk. One huge hand grabbed a fistful of Sam Wilkie's shirt and pulled him up until he was dancing on tiptoes. Wilkie's face went from a livid flush to a pasty white.

The glass in the office walls rattled with Burke's thundering voice. "Try this scenario, Wilkie. This afternoon I call a meeting of the board of directors. Monday morning when you come to work, your name is no longer on your office door."

Out in the newsroom, reporters were staring.

Burke put Wilkie down. The white-faced editor stepped over to a cooler and gulped some water. He ran trembling fingers through his hair and made an effort to straighten his tie. "All right, if you feel that way about it. We'll run a retraction."

"Page one."

"Yes," Wilkie said sourly. "Page one."

"Big headline."

"All right! Big headline."

"Something like, '*Courier* Apologizes for Unfair Character Assassination.'"

"Maybe you'd like to write the story?" Wilkie said sarcastically.

"I'm a cattleman, not a writer," Burke said. "But I can read. And what I read tomorrow better sound damn humble and apologetic. Do I make myself clear?"

"You make yourself clear," Wilkie muttered sullenly.

"Sometimes," Burke said to Kathy and Dak as they left the newspaper office, "You have to explain things to people in a way that they'll understand what you mean."

Chapter Twelve

Once they were out on the street, Burke told Kathy and Dak that he had to get back to his ranch and drove off in his truck.

Alone with Dak, Kathy felt suddenly self-conscious. "I—I need to get back to my office."

"Would you have time for a cup of coffee?" Dak asked. "There's something I want to talk to you about."

She consulted her watch. "Well . . . all right."

They crossed the street to the Henderson Café.

"This café used to stay open all night," Dak reminisced after they had found a booth and the waitress had set down two mugs of steaming coffee. "It was a hangout for our high school crowd. We'd come here after school proms.''

"These days the teen crowd hangs out at the mall.''

Her eyes were drawn to Dak who was gazing into his coffee as if deep in thought. He cleared his throat and glanced up, catching her gaze. She quickly looked away.

"Kathy,'' he said, "an awful lot of things have happened since Cliff Dunlap woke me up early this morning. It's pretty clear that I owe you an apology. I can see that I was wrong about your father using his influence to get you elected. It's obvious to me after what I saw this morning that you're doing it on your own.''

Kathy's gaze returned to Dak's face, to his eyes. "Thank you for telling me that, Dak,'' she said softly, her eyes alight. "I'd begun to have some doubts myself about Daddy, but he gave me his word and now I know he's keeping it.''

"Yes,'' Dak admitted. "And I feel sure if you win that you're going to run things your way. So, I can't see any point in my staying in the race.''

She stared at him for a moment, too shocked to reply. "Just what do you mean by that?''

"You know why I entered the race in the first place. I was tired of Burke Ayers running the town.''

"How do you feel about his daughter running the town?"

Dak grinned. "I think she'd do an outstanding job."

Kathy gave him an angry look. "Thanks for the vote of confidence, but Dak Roberts, I'll never forgive you if you drop out of this race."

He looked surprised. "I thought you'd be pleased. With me out of the way you're a shoo-in."

"I'd also never know for certain who would win," she said heatedly. "I want to get elected because the voters had a chance to judge us and decided they wanted me. I don't want to win by default! We have a television debate scheduled for Friday night. You'd better be there or I'll tell the whole town you turned chicken!"

A slow grin spread over Dak's tanned face. "All right. You asked for it. You might be sorry, though."

"No I won't. I'll mop up the floor with you!"

On Friday night they were seated on a set in the local television studio. A news anchorman served as moderator. When the program got underway, Dak announced that he had a statement to make before they began debating.

"I made it clear when I entered this race," he began, "that I wasn't running against Kathy Ayers so much as I was campaigning against her father, Burke

Ayers, who I felt had exerted too much political influence on this community over the years. I am now convinced that he is not involved politically in this race in any way. Kathy is running her own race and if she is elected mayor, she'll be serving with no outside influence.''

A genuine smile crossed Kathy's face. Debating with her good friend would not be easy, but she managed to put personal feelings aside. Then the debate got underway.

On the following Saturday, the voters of Endless, Texas, went to the polls to elect their mayor. It was a close race, but by nine o'clock that night the television station broadcast the projected winner. ''For the first time in the history of Endless, Texas, we have a woman mayor. Kathy Ayers!''

At Kathy's campaign headquarters, hysteria reigned—just the beginning of a wild victory party that would last into the small hours. Confetti and streamers flew through the air. Balloons were released. Champagne corks popped. Amidst all the confusion, a remote TV unit taped a victory speech. On the TV screen, she saw Dak Roberts give his brief concession speech. Tears welled in Kathy's eyes, blurring his image. In the midst of her happiness, she felt empty.

A few days later, after the hysteria of election night had subsided, Kathy was driving slowly through the streets of Endless on the way to her office when she passed a familiar sight—the municipal pool. She parked and walked across a grassy area to the pool and stood outside the high chain link fence, gazing at the activity around the pool. A flood of poignant memories engulfed her as she watched the teenagers splashing in the water and sunbathing. Wasn't it only yesterday that she had been one of them?

Suddenly, her breath caught. Her gaze was riveted on a stalwart figure—broad-shouldered, slim-hipped. The lifeguard was Dak! The same shock of dark hair, the golden body rippling with muscles.

But the young man turned. He might be today's Olympic material of a younger generation, but he wasn't Dak. It wasn't yesterday and she wasn't one of the giggling teenage girls casting adoring eyes at the handsome young guard.

She sighed and blinked away a tear.

"Feel like a swim?" a masculine voice said behind her.

With a gasp she whirled and looked into a pair of blue eyes. This time it was no illusion.

"Dak!" she stammered.

"I was in town taking care of some business," he explained. "I usually take this street going back to my place. I guess this old city park holds a lot of memories for me. Sometimes I stop for a few minutes and watch the kids having a good time. I couldn't believe my eyes when I saw you. Were you doing some reminiscing?''

"I guess so," she confessed, her cheeks flushing.

There was a moment of tense silence as she tried unsuccessfully to draw her eyes from the power of his gaze. Her look strayed over the handsome, rugged lines of his face, drinking in the beloved features that had filled so many of her dreams for so many years. Finally she stammered, "How's Joedy? I was so busy with the campaign the past two weeks I'm afraid I've been neglecting him."

"Yes, and he's not too happy about that. He wants you to see the buckle he won at the rodeo now that his name is engraved on it. Could you come out to the ranch tomorrow? I'll treat you to a picnic down at my creek."

"That sounds like fun."

"It will be."

There was another lengthy pause. Kathy was acutely aware that Dak was still holding her hands. "It's really good to see you again, Kathy, now that we're no longer political enemies."

With an effort, she drew her hands from his grasp. Her knees felt weak. "It—it turned out to be a friendly race," she reminded him.

There was a twinkle in Dak's eyes. "You weren't so friendly at that TV debate. You ripped me to shreds. Our local political analysts have decided it was that debate that won you the election."

"I warned you I'd mop up the floor with you," she reminded him. "But it was nothing personal." She hesitated. "Thank you for that statement you made before the debate, Dak. It meant a lot to me."

"I was just telling the truth. I guess when I first came back to Endless, I couldn't accept the fact that ten years had gone by and you were a woman. I kept seeing you as the teenager dominated by her father. I told you that if you proved me wrong, I'd admit it in a public speech. I was just fulfilling my promise."

"Well, I'll see you and Joedy tomorrow."

The next morning, dressed in blue jeans and Western boots, she rode to Dak's ranch. She and Joedy had a happy reunion. He proudly showed her the belt buckle that now was inscribed with his name.

"Joedy's been invited to spend the day with a friend," Dak explained as he saddled a horse. "They're picking him up in a little while."

"I'm glad to hear Joedy's making friends," Kathy said a little while later as she and Dak rode out of the ranch yard.

"Yes, it's another healthy sign that he's becoming a normal little boy again," Dak said happily. "He met a number of kids at the rodeo. Some of them have been coming over here and he's been visiting them."

They rode to the grassy spot on the creek that Dak had shown her the first time he took her on a tour of his ranch. They tied their horses on the bank shaded with great oak trees. Below, the stream bubbled over a graveled bed. Kathy took off her boots and waded in the shallow water while Dak leaned contentedly against a tree trunk and whittled on a twig, watching her.

At noon, a plume of dust coming down a dirt lane marked the approach of a pickup truck. "That'll be José Alemán bringing the picnic," Dak exclaimed. He closed his knife, rose and walked to the lane to flag down the cook. José, driving with a wild look in his eyes, was coming at breakneck speed, weaving and taking great bouncing leaps over hummocks in the road.

"Hope he isn't bringing any breakable dishes," Dak muttered.

By some miracle, the truck slid to a stop without turning over. The cook clambered from behind the wheel and bowed politely to Kathy before he busily transferred baskets of food from the pickup.

They spread the meal out on a white cloth. "What a feast!" Kathy gasped. There were appetizers, salad, fried chicken, loaves of homemade bread. In the center of the spread was a large chocolate cake.

"José, this is wonderful," Kathy exclaimed. "Thank you."

The cook stared at her blankly.

"You have to tell him in Spanish," Dak told her. "He doesn't understand English."

Kathy repeated her praise in Spanish.

José beamed and nodded, then got back in the truck and took off in a cloud of dust. Kathy watched the pickup bouncing wildly across the prairie. "I hope you've got that truck insured," she muttered.

Dak opened a chilled bottle of champagne and filled two thin-stemmed glasses. "This is my first chance to toast our new mayor. To a lovely lady mayor. Congratulations, Kathy." Dak raised his glass.

Dak's gaze centered on her in a way that made her heart pound. Quickly, she took a sip from her glass and put it down. "My, all that looks good. I'm famished."

"I told you the ride out here would give you an appetite," Dak laughed.

They sat around the picnic spread in the shade. Their dinner music was the bubbling of the stream and the prolonged cadence of cicadas.

"We'd—we'd better start back," she said nervously wiping her palms on her jeans. "It's a long ride to the house."

"Let's let our lunch settle," Dak said easily. "You might get a cramp riding on a full stomach."

I might get worse than that hanging around here alone with you, Kathy thought uneasily. But Dak refused to listen to her protests. He took her hand and led her to the edge of the bank. They settled in the soft grass with the creek just below them.

Kathy stretched out on her back, gazing up at the patches of sky she could see through the branches. She tried to concentrate on the scenery, but Dak's presence was too close for her to marshal her thoughts. His masculine scent made her senses reel and elevated her pulse rate. He was so close she could feel the warmth of his body.

Dak was propped on an elbow, gazing steadily down at her, disconcerting her even more. She shivered as he trailed a finger along the contour of her cheek. "You look lovely, lying there with the grass around you, Kathy," he said softly, "like a jewel in a velvet box."

"Dak—" She tried to sit up, but he gently placed a hand on her shoulder.

"Relax, Kathy."

"How can I, with your hand on my shoulder?"

His lips brushed her cheek.

"Dak," she said unsteadily, "please don't do that." Tears were filling her eyes.

"Why not?"

"Because it isn't fair. You have no right to—to—"

"To what? Make love to you?"

Her cheeks burned. "No. Yes. Oh, I don't know."

A smile tugged at Dak's lips. "This would be a lovely spot for it. There's no one around for miles. Just you and me, here, surrounded by nature."

"Dak, don't talk like that," she said, her voice growing thicker. Her breasts were rising and falling swiftly as desire, like a sudden flash fire, awakened in her.

"Kathy—"

"No, I won't listen to another word," she said, putting her hands over her ears. "You know I don't have a whole lot of self-control where you're concerned."

"Then let go of your self-control," he said softly.

His gentle kisses touched her forehead, her eyelids, her lips, her throat. He opened the top buttons of her blouse. She moaned as his lips found the soft valley between her breasts. Her fingers plowed into his hair. She gasped his name.

"Kathy, do you want to know what I said in one of those letters I wrote ten years ago?"

"What did you say?" she asked unsteadily.

"I asked you to marry me."

She swallowed a painful lump. "Oh, Dak—"

"Are you sorry you didn't get the letter?"

"Of course. It would have changed everything."

"What would you have replied?"

"Ten years ago? I'm sure I would have said yes."

"What if I were to ask the same question now?"

She sat up, looking at him solemnly. "Dak Roberts, are you proposing?"

"Yes. But things aren't the same as ten years ago. I have a son now."

"A son I adore."

"And who adores you."

Her heart was suddenly pounding wildly. "Dak, are you sure?"

"I've never been more sure of anything in my life, Kathy. I loved you ten years ago. I never stopped loving you. Do you still love me?"

Gazing into his eyes, she whispered, "Yes. I've always loved you, Dak. You were my first love, my hero. I never got over loving you...."

"Well, then?"

"Are you going to mind being married to a career woman, a lady mayor?"

"Not at all."

"Well then," she said softly, "I guess it's just a matter of breaking the news to Joedy that he's going to have a new mom and setting the date."

"Now is there any other reason we can't get married?"

She looked into his eyes, her heart filling with joy. "I can't think of any."

He gently pushed her back down on the grassy bed and kissed her. "Then let's see...where were we a few minutes ago?"

*   *   *   *   *

Silhouette Romance™

Legendary Lovers Trilogy

BY DEBBIE MACOMBER....

ONCE UPON A TIME, in a land not so far away, there lived a girl, Debbie Macomber, who grew up dreaming of castles, white knights and princes on fiery steeds. Her family was an ordinary one with a mother and father and one wicked brother, who sold copies of her diary to all the boys in her junior high class.

One day, when Debbie was only nineteen, a handsome electrician drove by in a shiny black convertible. Now Debbie knew a prince when she saw one, and before long they lived in a two-bedroom cottage surrounded by a white picket fence.

As often happens when a damsel fair meets her prince charming, children followed, and soon the two-bedroom cottage became a four-bedroom castle. The kingdom flourished and prospered, and between soccer games and car pools, ballet classes and clarinet lessons, Debbie thought about love and enchantment and the magic of romance.

One day Debbie said, "What this country needs is a good fairy tale." She remembered how well her diary had sold and she dreamed again of castles, white knights and princes on fiery steeds. And so the stories of Cinderella, Beauty and the Beast, and Snow White were reborn....

Look for Debbie Macomber's *Legendary Lovers* trilogy from Silhouette Romance: *Cindy and the Prince* (January, 1988); *Some Kind of Wonderful* (March, 1988); *Almost Paradise* (May, 1988). Don't miss them!

SRT-1

Silhouette Special Edition

NORA ROBERTS'S 50TH SILHOUETTE NOVEL

In May, SILHOUETTE SPECIAL EDITION celebrates Nora Roberts's "golden anniversary"— her 50th Silhouette novel!

The Last Honest Woman launches a three-book "family portrait" of entrancing triplet sisters. You'll fall in love with all THE O'HURLEYS!

The Last Honest Woman—May
Hardworking mother Abigail O'Hurley Rockwell finally meets a man she can trust...but she's forced to deceive him to protect her sons.

Dance to the Piper—July
Broadway hoofer Maddy O'Hurley easily lands a plum role, but it takes some fancy footwork to win the man of her dreams.

Skin Deep—September
Hollywood goddess Chantel O'Hurley remains deliberately icy...until she melts in the arms of the man she'd love to hate.

Look for THE O'HURLEYS! And join the excitement of Silhouette Special Edition!